The Untimely Journey
of Veronica T. Boone

The Untimely Journey of Veronica T. Boone

Part 1 - Laurentide

D. M. Sears

MacGregor Books
Washington DC MMXVIII

Cover art by Allison Mattice

ISBN: 099623151X
ISBN-13: 9780996231510
Library of Congress Control Number: 2017915422
MacGregor Books, Incorporated

Printed in the United States of America

Books by D.M. Sears
The Untimely Journey of Veronica T. Boone
The Manifest Destiny of Veronica T. Boone

For Elizabeth Jeanne,
who could give Molly a run for her money

With special thanks to
Alandra, Tayt, Greer,
Lady Eleanor, Kimberly, Matthew,
and Michael

Table of Contents

Preface

Houtzdale, Pennsylvania - 1893

Mr. T.D. Farnham walked quickly along the platform of the train station, his steps echoing on the wooden boards. Around him was a flurry of activity. The third-largest circus in the country was getting ready to travel. People ran to and fro, horses whinnied, and carriages creaked as they rolled into place. It wasn't quite chaos but it was close.

Farnham wore black boots, a frock coat, and a top hat. He slapped a riding crop against his thigh as he wondered how to make everyone move faster.

"Get those animals loaded, Peters!" he barked to a dusty man tugging on two Bactrian camels. "We don't have all day... Watkins, you told me the ponies would be ready to go aboard at 9:30. It's now 9:45 and they're still in the corral! We're not running a boarding house here – if you can't do it yourself then get some kinkers to help you... You there, Oscar! What's taking so long with that boxcar? The door's stuck? You're the Human Cannonball, confound it – blast it open if you have to!... I want to be out of here at noon, people. At noon! Am I the only one with a sense of urgency around here?"

People jumped at his orders. When the circus was underway and customers packed the seats under the big top, T.D. Farnham was "Ringmaster Ned," the jolly, friendly host of Farnham & Main's Spectacular Circus – The Greatest Show on Earth! But when the performances were over and the big tent had come down, he was *Mister* Farnham, circus manager, and there was nothing jolly about him then.

It was a big job, running a circus. Someone needed to make the decisions: who to hire, who to fire, who should get paid and how much, when the show would open, when it would close, what towns to visit and how to get customers in the door. Someone needed to get the show into a town and then out again. Someone needed to organize the 120 acrobats, trapeze artists, carnival freaks, animal trainers, horseback riders, clowns, candy butchers, kinkers, and jugglers so they could pack up the entire circus in just a few hours. And someone needed to make sure the train was loaded on time.

"Hercules," Farnham yelled to a huge man with rippling muscles who was helping to herd a baby elephant onto a train car. "What are you doing? If Jimbo steps on your foot I won't have a strongman in my circus. Move out of the way and let the animal trainers handle the elephants. Go find something to pick up."

"Mrs. Burkinov, what are you doing here?" he said a few minutes later to a woman walking along the platform. Mrs. Burkinov wore a blue dress and carried a parasol. She also had a beard covering half her face. "You should be on board with the rest of the sideshow performers."

"Ya, boot I cannot fahnd mah hoosband," the woman pouted in a thick Russian accent.

Farnham pointed to the end of the train. "Your husband The Tattooed Man was down there a while ago. He's helping Sinbad the Snake Charmer catch rats."

"But vy do they vant to catch rats?"

"To feed the snakes, I suppose. How do I know? But I would appreciate it if you would find your husband and Sinbad both and tell them to get on board. We're on a tight schedule. I want to be on our way to Lewistown in two hours."

"Ya, I vill do that," The Bearded Woman replied and hurried off.

Farnham kept walking to the end of the platform. There he hopped down to the ground and continued along the tracks until he reached the front of the train.

The locomotive had seen better days. The engine was normally decorated in red and gold but now the paint was faded. The wheels were rusty and the smokestack was crooked. The name of Farnham's business partner – *WALTER L. MAIN*, written below the smokestack – was even missing letters. Farnham wanted to fix up the whole train but that cost money. To get money he needed to put on more shows. To put on more shows they needed to get out of this blasted station...

"Is everything satisfactory, Mr. Croswell?" he called up to the cab.

The old engineer there looked down. "Ay, sir! We're running fine. The *Walter Main* don't look like much but he's as reliable as a banker's watch."

Farnham studied his own pocket watch. "I'm glad to hear it," he sighed. "At least that's one thing that won't hold us up."

Behind him the rest of the circus was not so organized. The Bengal tiger was safely in his cage but the African lions were still sitting in crates on the platform. Jimbo was moving slowly up the ramp to his car – Jimbo was never a problem – but those flighty Shetland ponies were still in the corral! And nobody had yet found two of his clowns. They had gone into town the night before and nobody had seen them since. Farnham shook his head – if those clowns showed up late he would make them shovel elephant poop for a week.

"Mr. Farnham! Mr. Farnham!"

Tommy O'Toole came running up. Tommy was a midget who was in a carnival act with Amazonia, the tallest woman in the world. He also worked as Mr. Farnham's assistant.

"What is it, Tommy? Did you find the clowns?"

"No, sir. Nobody has seen them."

"Well, if they miss the train they're fired."

"Yes, sir. But Mr. Farnham..."

"Good. How about Mungabo the Beast Tamer? Is he still mad at everyone or is he going to get on the train?"

"Both, sir. He's mad at everyone *and* he is on the train. But now his monkeys are refusing to board. He says they want more bananas or they won't go on to the next town." Tommy pointed to a troop of monkeys who were climbing all over the roof of the train station.

Farnham was unimpressed. "You tell Mungabo to talk some sense into those idiots before twelve o'clock or I'll leave them behind."

"Yes, sir. But..."

"And another thing..."

"Sir, let me finish! There are two men who want to see you."

"Two men?" Farnham looked along the platform. The station was hung with red, white, and blue bunting in honor of Decoration Day but by the station door were two men and a tall, gangly girl who were not dressed nearly so colorfully. The men wore wool waist-coats, workers' pants, and cloth caps. One had a sash around his waist. The girl was dressed all in black with a feather sticking out of her hat. The men started walking his way.

"Who are they?" he demanded. "They're too scruffy to be from the bank."

"No, sir."

"They don't look like railroad inspectors, either."

"No, sir. They wouldn't say who they are," Tommy insisted. "But they want to talk to you."

"Not now, Tommy. We've got to get this show on the road. Besides, if they're looking for jobs I don't need anybody."

"Sir, they don't want work. They want to buy the train."

Farnham stopped. "They want what?"

"That's what they said."

"That's ridiculous. Tell them it's not for sale."

"I did! They said they don't care. They want to buy it."

Farnham slapped his riding crop angrily against his leg.

"Darn it, Tommy! I don't have time for such guff. We have a show tomorrow night in Lewistown. Mr. Main is ahead of us putting up posters and selling tickets. That's money we can't afford to lose."

"But what should I tell them?" Tommy asked nervously as the men came closer.

"Tell them to get lost or you'll bite their kneecaps. I don't care what you tell them, just don't let them waste my time."

But it was too late. The two men intercepted Farnham as he walked to the baggage car.

"We heard your train is for sale," one man snarled. He had a dirty face and smoked a cigarette.

"You heard wrong," Farnham snapped. "We're a circus and the *Walter Main* is a circus train. It's not for sale."

"We'll make you a good offer."

"You could offer me tea with the Queen of England and it wouldn't make any difference."

"We'll pay you ten thousand dollars."

Farnham's jaw dropped. "Ten thousand dollars? Why, the whole circus isn't worth that much!"

"We don't want the whole circus," the second man said. He crossed his arms and glared at Farnham. "We just want the train."

T.D. Farnham rubbed his chin. He was a smart enough businessman to know when he was being conned. There was something fishy about these fellows.

"Who are you?" he asked. "Why do you want a train?"

"None of your business," the man with the cigarette scowled.

"It is my business if you're going to throw around money like John D. Rockefeller. And where did you get ten thousand dollars?"

"You're asking too many questions, circus man. Just sell us the train."

"No, you can't have it."

"Oh, I think we can. Sign here." Cigarette Man held out a piece of paper with Farnham's name already printed on the bottom.

"I'm not signing anything," Farnham barked.

He tried to push past the two men but they shoved him against the side of the baggage car.

"You'll sign," the man with the sash snarled. "Or we'll..."

His words were choked off as suddenly he was lifted into the air. Cigarette Man, too, found himself off the ground and dangling two feet above the dirt.

"Are these men bothering you, Mr. Farnham?" Hercules asked. The circus strongman held up the two thugs as though they were mice he had found in a trap. The men struggled but Hercules didn't budge. Other circus workers gathered around.

"Yes, they are!" Farnham exclaimed. "They're hoodlums! Criminals! Throw them out in the street. Wait! I have a better idea. Hercules, the ponies should be out of their corral by now.

There must be a fine pile of horse poop left behind. Do me a favor and deliver these two ruffians to a nice tall stinking pile of manure."

"Yes, sir, Mr. Farnham," Hercules replied. He walked off with the two men crying and kicking their feet.

"How about that?" Farnham huffed. "Have you ever heard anything so bizarre?"

"No, sir, Mr. Farnham," said Tommy. "I never have."

"Neither have I. Well, forget about it. Everyone get back to work! I want to be on the road in" – he checked his pocket watch – "ninety-two minutes. Now move!"

Two hours later the *Walter Main* circus train pulled out of the Houtzdale station. T.D. Farnham breathed a sigh of relief. Sitting in the lead car he checked off items on a long list.

"The crocodiles are on board?" he asked Tommy.

"Yes, sir," his assistant replied. "I saw them myself."

"The kangaroo rodeo, the dancing pythons, and both sacred cows?"

"Check, check, and check, sir. Sinbad has the cows in the same car as the gorilla."

Mr. Farnham looked up. "The sacred cows are in the same car as the Man-Slayer?" he asked, shivering just thinking about Mungabo's scariest pet.

"Yes, sir. Mungabo told the Man-Slayer that if he eats the cows he'll end up in a zoo."

"I'm not sure that will make the cows feel any safer," Mr. Farnham sighed. "But he's the expert so it's his decision. Oh, one more thing: did the clowns ever show up?"

"Yes, sir. I saw them jump on the caboose just as we left."

"The caboose? Well, it serves them right. They can ride back there with the brakeman instead of in their cabin." Farnham leaned back in his seat and looked out the window. The farmland outside was lush and green. It had been an unusually fine May. "Tommy, we can finally relax. We have nineteen train cars loaded with the most spectacular circus in the whole country so let's celebrate and enjoy the trip to Lewistown. If everything goes well we'll be there before midnight tonight."

Up in the locomotive Mr. Croswell guided the *Walter Main* through the countryside of Pennsylvania. For two hours everything was peaceful: the engine chugged along and steam rose from the stack in great clouds to trail over the cars behind.

It was only as they drove into the Allegheny Mountains that Mr. Croswell grew worried.

"Ease up on the fuel," he told his fireman, who stood behind him shoveling coal into the firebox. "We need to go slow now. Too much speed and we won't stay on the tracks."

They climbed into the Lewistown Pass. The hills grew steep and the turns became sharp. The *Walter Main* huffed its way carefully up the slope.

They reached the top of the pass without a hitch but as the train started down the back side of the mountain it picked up speed. Mr. Croswell blew three short *toots* on the whistle.

"That's our signal to the caboose," he told the fireman. "The fellows there control the brakes so they had better be awake."

But the train continued to go faster. Mr. Croswell blew the whistle again.

"What's the matter with those guys?" He leaned out his window and looked back. Far in the rear he saw someone waving. "They're awake at least. But that looks like a clown. What's a clown doing in the caboose? And why aren't they putting on the brakes?"

The train continued rolling faster. The hills above Lewistown fell sharply into a valley and the rails switched back and forth on their way down. Even the wide turns could be tricky if a train carried too much speed. Mr. Croswell worried most about the curve at the bottom of the pass, the one called The Horseshoe.

"We're going too fast," he fretted. "The wheels are getting shaky. We'll never pass The Horseshoe like this."

In the middle of the cab was a huge lever that controlled the brakes of the locomotive. Mr. Croswell grabbed it and pulled. The brakes squealed but the train only slowed a little bit. The weight of nineteen cars was too much for the locomotive to stop on its own. Their brakes were controlled by the caboose. Pretty soon the *Walter Main* began to lean as it went around curves.

"There's something wrong!" he cried as they rushed down the mountain. "Go find out what's happening. We'll never stay on the tracks at this speed."

The fireman dropped his shovel and climbed to the top of the locomotive. The only way to get to the caboose now was to run along the top of the train. It was dangerous but this was an emergency.

Mr. Croswell grabbed the big lever and pulled again – it was no use. Trains go from the front but they stop from the rear. He needed someone in the caboose to apply the brakes.

Mr. Croswell would have been more frightened if he could have seen what was going on inside the caboose. There the real brakeman lay unconscious on the floor. Two men wearing clown costumes and smelling strongly of horse poop stood over him.

"Good thing those clowns passed out in the saloon last night," the first man laughed. He pulled off his rubber nose and threw it on the floor. Then he lit a cigarette. "They'll wonder where their costumes are when they wake up."

The other clown had a red sash tied to his costume. "That ringmaster should have sold us the train," he growled. "Now he'll learn not to mess with us."

With that, the men went out the back door. The whole train rocked and tipped. Up ahead they saw the dreaded Horseshoe curve approaching.

"Har-har," the one with the sash said. "I hope that Hercules guy has an elephant land on him when this train goes off the rails."

With that, the men jumped. They landed in high grass, unhurt. By then the *Walter Main* was entering The Horseshoe. They could see the fireman running along the top of the train but he had not yet reached the caboose. And now he was too late.

From the locomotive came a last, piercing wail of the steam whistle as Mr. Croswell warned everyone to hang on.

PART 1

Laurentide

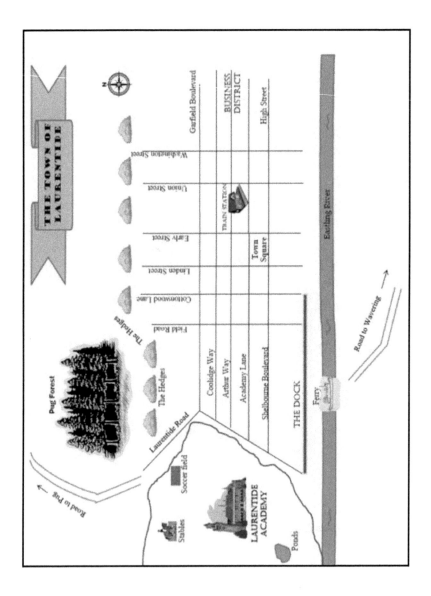

CHAPTER 1

The Academy

Laurentide, Ohio - Today

THE CLOCK ON the wall in Mr. Willis-Biggs' fourth period history class ticked backward. Molly hated it when it did that.

The clock hung high on the wall near the door. It had a white face and black numbers and two fat hands that hardly ever seemed to budge. Only when a minute had almost passed did the hands move at all. And then they moved backward! Not much: they backed up just a little before jumping forward. But Molly hated the clock anyway. Clocks aren't supposed to go backward. Every time this one did, it made her think time was going in reverse and she would be stuck in history class forever.

Which was a shame because Molly didn't hate history. She liked it. She liked school, too, and she loved her school in particular, the Laurentide Academy, that wonderful old building with its towering halls and antique desks and bright windows that looked out on acres and acres of fields and trees.

It was just that Mr. Willis-Biggs was BORING. He was a nice man but he talked about things that put Molly to sleep. Things like the Great Depression and World War I and the Constitution. Her eyelids drooped just hearing the words. And his voice didn't help. It was deep and soft like the rumble of a faraway train. And what was up with his name, anyway? Was he Mr. Willis or Mr.

Biggs? Couldn't he decide? Molly wasn't sure she trusted people with two last names, especially people who mumbled like a faraway train.

That's why she spent so much time staring at the clock. Staring at it, hating it, wanting it to move.

Miraculously, on this day the hands finally budged. They leaped forward to the top of the hour, the bell rang, and Molly grabbed her backpack and was out the door.

"Excuse me, pardon me, on your left..."

She hurried through Students Hall as students streamed from classrooms. Laurentide Academy had *halls*, not corridors, and Students Hall was the grandest of them all. It was tall and wide with fat pillars down the middle and enormous bookcases along the walls. Above the bookcases were portraits of famous students. Each portrait was accompanied by a small shelf holding a shiny Memorial Cup to honor the year that student had graduated. Molly didn't know why the students were being honored. The only reason she ever noticed them was because they all looked strong and positive and very determined, which was unusual for people her age. On days when she didn't feel all that smart she took comfort walking in the hall and having all those former students look down at her with their confident smiles. It made her feel stronger herself.

Across the ceiling were banners. Carpet covered the floor. Grand staircases rose next to tall windows with colored glass. When it rained, the windows were like a waterfall and made the hall shimmer in rainbow colors.

But right now Molly didn't notice the paintings, the banners, or the rainbows. She dashed to the stairs. Down one level she ran, through the Gallery, across Founders Hall, into the courtyard with its fountain shaped like a clock tower with a strange dome on top, and up the path to the Dining Room.

"You're not going to believe this!" her best friend Kate said two minutes later as Molly slid into the seat next to her. Kate always said that whenever she had news.

"Peter Dumfrey has been fired from the pet shop?" Molly guessed.

"No, silly. Peter's dad *owns* the pet shop. He wouldn't fire his own son."

"He would if he knew Peter brings animals to school and sticks them in girls' backpacks to scare them," Molly insisted.

"He doesn't stick them in all girls' backpacks," Kate corrected her. "Only yours."

"Well, if he does it again I'll tear his arms off! Then his dad will have to fire him because he won't be able to pick up any of the animals in the shop."

"Be nice. He likes you."

"He does not! You heard what happened in art class yesterday – I reached into my bag for a pencil and touched a kinkajou. A kinkajou! I didn't even know what a kinkajou was until it bit me. I screamed louder than I've ever screamed in my life!"

"I know," Kate said. "I heard you."

"Were you in the next classroom?"

"No, I was at the other end of the building."

"Really? You could hear me that far away?"

"People *in town* heard you, Molly. Old Mrs. Walters down by the train station called up to the academy to see if everyone was okay. And she's been deaf for years."

"Well," insisted Molly, "I had every reason to scream. I touched a kinkajou."

"But kinkajous are cute."

"They're cute when you're cuddling one and scratching it behind the ears. They're NOT cute when you don't know it's in your bag and it bites you!"

Kate waved her hands.

"Molly, you're getting me off the topic," she pleaded. "I don't want to talk about Peter and his pets. I want to talk about what I heard in the dentist office this morning."

"Why were you in the dentist office this morning?"

"Because I ate almonds. I'm not supposed to eat nuts while I have braces but I did and one of them got caught under a wire so my mom took me to Doctor Payne to get it fixed."

"Why do you go to him?"

"To Doctor Payne? Because he's a dentist."

"But his name is Doctor Payne. *Payne*. Like pain, p-a-i-n. I wouldn't want to go to a dentist whose name was Doctor Pain. I would always think of him as Doctor Painful. Or Doctor Sore. Or Doctor Ouch-That-Really-Hurts..."

"Molly! Will you stop changing the subject? I'm trying to tell you something."

"Oh, sorry."

"I swear, you have such a skill at making people forget what they're talking about. You never focus."

"Really, I'm sorry. Sometimes my mind just goes off in different directions. So tell me, what did you hear at Doctor Painful's office?"

Kate turned serious. "Jeannie Anderson was in the other chair. You know, her mom and dad are friends with the mayor? Well, she had a big plaster mold stuck in her face so they could make her a new retainer and while everyone was waiting for it to dry her mom was whispering with Doctor Payne. They were talking about school. About Laurentide."

"And?"

"Molly, they're going to fire Mr. Gladden!"

"What?!" Molly couldn't believe her ears. "But he's the nicest headmaster ever. When I took the test to get into the school I was so nervous I forgot to bring pencils so he loaned me his right out of his own pocket. If he hadn't done that I wouldn't be here today. They couldn't fire him, could they?"

"I don't know," Kate admitted. "I didn't hear everything. But they said something about a woman from Pug who is coming to replace him."

"Pug?" Molly repeated. "That's impossible, Kate. Pug is five miles away. You know as well as I do that the Headmaster of Laurentide Academy is always someone from the town of Laurentide. It's the same for students and teachers. To be at Laurentide you have to live in Laurentide."

"That's why it's such big news."

"We don't even accept students from Wavering and they're just down the river. And they're not nearly as unpleasant as people from Pug."

"I know. It's awful."

"Besides, Pug is such a depressing town. My mother says all the good stores closed because no one there ever wants to work. They just want you to pay them for doing nothing."

"That's true," Kate agreed. "We used to go to the movie theater in Pug but it got so dirty we stopped. And people there were rude."

"It went out of business," Molly said. "So did the ice cream parlor. My dad said the owners got tired of people wanting everything for free. They moved to Wavering instead where nobody can ever make up their mind but at least they work."

"Pug people do seem to want everyone else to do everything for them. That's why I can't imagine anyone from there coming to Laurentide."

"I don't believe it," Molly declared. "The Trustees of the Academy have never let anyone from outside the town be headmaster. Jeannie must not have heard correctly."

"Maybe not," Kate said. "But if you don't believe her, just wait until tomorrow."

"Why? What happens then?"

"I don't know. But Jeannie said something about an announcement. And Molly?"

"Yes?"

Kate frowned. "Jeannie sounded worried. I hope the news doesn't get any worse."

The news didn't get any worse but Molly's day sure did. In her Latin class everyone laughed at her. She was at the chalkboard writing a sentence when suddenly she thought she saw her backpack move. Kate had warned her that Peter Dumfrey was going to put a snake in her bag so immediately she ran over and started kicking it, yelling "take that!..and that!.." But Peter wasn't even in her Latin class and it turned out the backpack only had her books and a peach she had saved from lunch. All Molly did was smash the peach.

Then just before leaving for home there was an announcement that final exams would happen on Thursday of next week. That was four days early! Now Molly had even less time to study. She had hoped that Mr. Willis-Biggs would move the History test *back* a few days, not forward, because then it might give Molly's father time to return from his business trip and help her understand all those people and events from the past that Mr. Willis-Biggs said were important. But now there was no way her dad would be home in time. And with her mother up in Chicago visiting her grandparents, Molly didn't have anyone to complain to.

Well, that wasn't quite true because she could always complain to Aunt Marcy, but Aunt Marcy wasn't any fun to complain to. She was always happy and optimistic and would simply tell Molly not to worry, that things would sort themselves out. That didn't help at all. When Molly worried about something, she wanted people to say, "Oh, yes, Molly. You're right. That is the most horrible, difficult thing to deal with." She didn't want to hear that her concerns were nothing. And besides, Aunt Marcy couldn't help Molly study. Aunt Marcy was like most people in that she thought history started the day she was born. Since Aunt Marcy wasn't very old that meant there was a lot of history she simply didn't know.

So when she walked home from the Academy that afternoon Molly felt out of sorts. Her parents were gone, kind Mr. Gladden was being fired, she had a history test to study for, and she had looked silly in her Latin class. She was so busy thinking about her rotten day that she didn't pay attention to where she was going.

"Oh no," she sighed, finally looking up. "I've gone right past my own house."

She had walked to the railroad tracks near the town square. The tracks were rusty and covered in weeds. A huge oak tree leaned over the spot where they ended. The railroad didn't come to Laurentide anymore. All that was left was a short stretch of rails that ran from the oak tree to the Union Street station.

And the station wasn't much to look at, either. It was abandoned except for one corner where Mrs. Walters ran her coffee shop. Most of the windows were boarded up. The ticket booth was closed. The roof lacked shingles and pigeons lived in the gutters. The clock tower looked ready to fall over. The clock itself was stuck at noon (or midnight) and had been as long as Molly could remember. One lonely old passenger car sat on rusted tracks next to the platform but even if there had been a locomotive to pull it they couldn't have gone anywhere because the tracks ended just past the cafe.

Molly wandered around but the station depressed her more than she already was. She walked back up to Linden Street and went home. Aunt Marcy was there, as happy as ever. Molly told her about Mr. Gladden and Latin class and the woman from Pug, and as always Aunt Marcy smiled and patted Molly's hand and said that everything would sort itself out.

Molly wanted to believe her but when she went to sleep that night she had trouble closing her eyes. She lay in her bed thinking of the clock in her history class and wondering why it was so odd. And just before she fell asleep she thought of something else.

Who was the woman from Pug?

CHAPTER 2

The Woman from Pug

As KATE HAD promised, on Wednesday there was an announcement that all students would report to the auditorium after fourth period.

Before then, Molly and Kate escaped outside to talk. They walked around the Academy grounds and were on their way back inside when Peter Dumfrey trotted up.

"Don't even think of touching my backpack," Molly warned him.

Peter laughed. "No kinkajous today," he said. "I was looking for Kate, actually. She always knows what's going on."

"But why would she tell you anything?" Molly asked. "Why don't you mind your own business?"

"Oh, it's alright," Kate said. "I tell Peter everything."

"You do? Why?"

"Well, he...um...he needs to know things. He spends all his free time working so if I didn't tell him what was going on he wouldn't know."

"That's right," said Peter, sticking his tongue out at Molly. "And today I was wondering if Kate had heard anything about the new Headmaster."

"Headmistress," Kate corrected him. "It's a woman from Pug, that's all I know."

"But why?" Peter asked. "Why from Pug? And why a woman?"

"What's wrong with having a woman as Headmaster?" Molly demanded.

"Nothing," said Peter. "But we've never had a woman as Headmaster. Not since Miss Shelbourne started the school and that's over a hundred years ago."

"Well, we can have one now," Kate insisted. "It just can't be someone from Pug."

"Maybe Mr. Gladden can explain things," Molly suggested, but as she spoke their conversation was interrupted by two cars that drove through the Academy gates. The cars were black with dark windows and didn't look like anything anyone drove in Laurentide.

The cars stopped at the front of the school. The driver of the first one hopped out and scurried around to open the passenger door. Out stepped a tall woman with a long face. She wore a black pantsuit and a black hat with a feather sticking out of it. Other people got out of the second car and gathered around the woman. Together they hurried up the steps.

"I hope that's not the woman from Pug," Peter said. "She looks like a stork. A mean, black stork."

"Why would anyone want someone like that instead of Mr. Gladden?" Molly wondered. "Kate, make sure you sit with me in the auditorium, okay?"

"Okay."

"I'll save you a seat if you want, Molly," Peter offered.

"Eww," Molly replied. "Don't you come anywhere near me, Peter Dumfrey. And if you try to touch my backpack," she said as he raised a hand to pat her on the shoulder, "I'll kick you so hard you'll have to crawl around the pet shop on your knees."

"Jeez, you don't appreciate a good joke. I promise, I won't put anything at all in your backpack today." Peter turned to go back to the building. "But maybe we should all be nice to each other from now on," he suggested. "If that woman is going to be our new Headmaster, something tells me we're going to need all the friends we can get."

He ran off. From inside the building Molly and Kate heard the bell.

"He's right," Kate said. "All of us students should stick together until we see what this woman is like. We may have to be nice to people we normally don't like – including Maddie with all of her gossip, and Devon, and even Peter..."

Molly started to agree but suddenly she felt something move in her pocket. She reached in and pulled out a yellow tree frog.

"Yaaiieee!!" she shrieked, and threw the frog into a pansy bed.

Kate covered her mouth and tried not to laugh as Molly hopped around in fright. When she finally calmed down she growled, "Maddie and her gossip I can handle. Devon isn't so bad even if he does smell like onions. But Peter Dumfrey? I really don't like that boy."

The auditorium was packed. Every seat was taken. Molly noticed that it wasn't just students in the room. Mr. Van Helsing was there, and Mrs. Walters and her husband, and so was Doctor Robert Shelbourne, who was one of only two descendants of Lady Elizabeth Shelbourne, the founder of the Academy.

On the stage two people sat in comfortable chairs. One was Mayor Smolt, a man Molly only knew from the Independence Day parade where he always rode in the first car and waved to people as though he knew them. Molly's dad said the mayor was always making promises to people and that's why they voted for him. (He never kept his promises but that didn't seem to bother most folks. They liked being promised things so they voted for him.) Molly didn't know anything about the mayor but he had a fake smile that she found creepy.

The other person was the tall lady from the black car. She still wore her hat with the long red feather and she looked out across the auditorium with impatience.

Mayor Smolt rose from his seat.

"Ladies and gentlemen, thank you for being here today," he began. "As some of you know, there have been some unexpected departures from the Academy Board of Trustees in recent months. Mr. Ashburn chose to retire, and Mrs. Edith Kaufmann also chose to move on to other things..."

"Meaning she was forced out!" someone shouted.

"Excuse me, excuse me," Mayor Smolt said quickly. "If anyone has anything to say, let him raise his hand. This is not a shouting match. And no, Mrs. Kaufmann was not forced out. The Board became aware of some...shall we say...*irregularities* in her personal finances and thought it would be best if she stepped down while those were sorted out."

There was a gasp from the crowd. Edith Kaufmann and her husband were owners of the famous K&G supermarkets. They lived in a simple house over on Field Road and everybody knew them.

"What exactly are you saying?" a gentleman by the wall asked. Molly thought it was Mr. Holmes, a lawyer who had an office across the street from Mrs. Walter's coffee shop.

"I'm saying," Mayor Smolt said, "that when it comes to Laurentide Academy it is important to avoid any impression that things are not being done absolutely according to the Trust, honestly and..." he glanced toward the lady in black "...and *fairly*." She nodded and smiled but to Molly her smile looked as though the stork was chewing on a lemon.

"And what about the other trustees?" someone called out. "What about Mr. Springer?"

"Mr. Springer went on a long vacation," Mayor Smolt explained.

"But why did he just disappear?"

"I don't know. He just told me he needed a vacation."

"I didn't hear that," Doctor Shelbourne said loudly. "Alan Springer is my cousin and he never said anything to me."

"Maybe you should talk to your cousin more often," the mayor suggested.

"And Mrs. Haizlip?" another voice called.

"As you know," Mayor Smolt said, "Mrs. Haizlip and her husband own several car dealerships. She told me that pressures of the business have caused her a great deal of stress. She said she needed some time off."

"Another vacation?" Mr. Holmes asked, clearly not believing a word of it.

"Exactly," said Mayor Smolt.

"Why is it that none of us have heard any of this before?" Mr. Van Helsing called out. "I know everyone on the Board of Trustees and none of them ever mentioned anything to me about wanting to leave. They just disappeared."

People around the room agreed with that. Laurentide was a small town. Everyone pretty much knew everyone.

"Perhaps," suggested Mayor Smolt, "they thought their reasons for leaving were a private affair and none of your business."

"Oooh dear," Kate whispered. "That was a smackdown."

Molly agreed. She felt uncomfortable listening to the adults in the room argue even though she wanted to hear what Mayor Smolt had to say. Clearly he was leading up to something.

"But leaving the Board is not a private affair," Mr. Van Helsing gently corrected the mayor. "These people have a responsibility to the Academy. They are trustees who have sworn to uphold the Academy Trust."

"Ah, yes," Mayor Smolt continued. "And that brings us to the matter of the Trust. With the, ah, *unexpected* departures of Mr. Ashburn, Mrs. Kaufmann, Mr. Springer, and Mrs. Haizlip, that left only Mr. Gladden and myself as duly constituted members of the Board. Therefore...uh, uh, yes?"

A small hand waved from the third row. It belonged to Peter Dumfrey.

"Where is Mr. Gladden?" Peter asked.

That was a good question. Mr. Gladden was always there for important announcements.

"Mr. Gladden resigned suddenly this week," Mayor Smolt began to explain but then had to stop when a chorus of disbelief arose from the crowd. "But...but...please listen, ladies and gentlemen... please listen. But he left a note and asked me to pass on to you his full support for whatever the rest of the Board of Trustees decide to do in his absence."

When the hubbub died down, Mrs. Walters was the first one to speak.

"But the only one left on the Board then," she said to Mayor Smolt, "is you."

Mayor Smolt smiled and smoothed his hair. "Why, yes. And that brings us to the reason I have called this meeting. To help me with the important task of leading Laurentide Academy, and to ensure that operations continue in the spirit of the Trust, I have decided to appoint a new Headmaster as quickly as possible to replace Mr. Gladden. Fortunately I was able to find someone very close by and on such short notice, a well-respected community organizer from our neighbors in Pug. Please join me in giving a warm Laurentide Academy welcome to Ms. Ursula Bamcroft!"

Mayor Smolt clapped as the woman in black stood up. No one else joined him.

The angry stork held her nose high, looking out at the audience. The students, teachers, and townspeople stared back.

"Good people of Laurentide," Ms. Bamcroft began, "*thank you* for appointing me Headmaster of Laurentide Academy."

"We didn't," someone grumbled.

Ms. Bamcroft scowled and tried to see who had spoken. When she couldn't, she put the lemony smile back on her face and tried again. "I won't take up your valuable time with a long speech. I just want you to know that as Headmaster I take my responsibilities *very* seriously, and my every effort will be dedicated to fixing the problems that have troubled the Academy for a long time. Of course by that I mean its lack of fairness and equality."

"Huh?" Molly whispered to Kate. "What's she talking about?"

"Since its very beginning over 100 years ago," Ms. Bamcroft said, "Laurentide Academy has been a good school for some but not for all. The hard-working children of Pug, for example, have never been allowed to attend Laurentide."

"That's because they have their own school in Pug," interrupted Mrs. Walters. "They can attend Laurentide if they move to Laurentide."

"I am speaking now!" Ms. Bamcroft shouted. "You will allow me to speak! Ahem, as I was saying, the children of Pug are not allowed to attend Laurentide Academy and that is not fair. Also," she added before Mrs. Walters could interrupt again, "some children get good grades at the Academy and some students do not. That is not fair. There are other things that are unfair here and I mean to fix them all. Now, I know some of you don't like change. But change is progress and my changes will bring progress to Laurentide. I promise you that if you don't like the changes, you don't have to accept them. If you like your classes, you can keep your classes. If you like your teachers, you can keep your teachers. But let me be clear: as your Headmaster, I intend to transform Laurentide Academy and make it a better, fairer place for everyone!"

With that, she was gone. Ursula Bamcroft turned and stalked off the stage without taking a single question. Mayor Smolt went with her and so did the little men who had followed her from the car. The students and teachers and everyone else in the auditorium were left to look at each other and wonder what had just happened.

CHAPTER 3

Strangeness

WHAT HAPPENED APPEARED to be a takeover of the Academy by the woman from Pug and her helper, the mayor. The adults started talking all at once, the students rushed back to their classrooms, and all in all it was the strangest day Molly had ever experienced.

But stranger things continued to happen. On her way home Molly tried to follow Peter Dumfrey. She wanted to punch him for putting the frog in her pocket but he gave her the slip. The last she saw of him was in the town square where he went into the Van Helsing antique shop.

Then on Thursday after school Molly went shopping with Aunt Marcy at the K&G grocery store and everyone there acted weirdly. When Molly pointed out that the store was out of corn flakes, Aunt Marcy claimed not to know what corn flakes were.

"What do you mean, what are corn flakes?" Molly laughed. "They're corn flakes. Dad only eats corn flakes for breakfast but there aren't any here on the shelf."

"I have no idea what you're talking about," Aunt Marcy replied. "Corn flakes? Like, flakes of corn? How do you flake corn? Just get him some Cheerios or granola or something."

"He won't eat Cheerios or granola," Molly reminded her aunt. "He only eats corn flakes." She asked a clerk but the clerk also said she had never heard of corn flakes. The manager said the same thing. Molly thought they were all playing a joke on her but couldn't figure out why.

But the very strangest thing happened in math class on Friday morning. Molly arrived to find a substitute teacher, a stout woman with heavy shoes that clumped when she walked. There were also three new kids in the class – two boys and a girl who Molly had never seen before. They weren't wearing school uniforms and one of the boys was sleeping at his desk.

"Where's Mr. Donovan?" Molly asked.

"He's been re-assigned," the woman said sharply. "Clear your desk!"

The woman gave the class a quiz. No problem: Molly liked math and went through the ten questions quickly. When the whole class had finished – except for the sleeping boy who never woke up – the teacher graded the quizzes and handed them back. Molly had done all ten problems correctly. She smiled...until she noticed her grade.

"Um, excuse me," she raised her hand. "Ma'am, you only gave me a score of 80."

"That's right," the woman replied.

"Shouldn't it be a 100?" Molly asked. "All my answers are correct."

"No, you get an 80," the teacher answered. The woman snatched Molly's quiz from her hand. "You have all your answers correct but Sarah here only got half of her answers right. So I took two of your correct answers and gave them to her. So you have 80 points instead of 100, and she has 70 instead of 50. That's more fair."

"Huh?" Molly asked.

A boy by the window raised his hand. "Ma'am, I got all the problems right, too, but you only gave me a 50. Not even an 80."

The teacher nodded. "That's because Felix here didn't get any of his questions right," she explained, tapping the sleeping boy. "It wouldn't be fair for him to get a zero so I gave him some of your points. Now you have a 50 and he has a 50."

"But he's asleep!" the boy by the window exclaimed.

"That's no reason why he should be punished," the teacher snapped. "Do you think you're better than him?"

"Um, no. But he didn't even take the test! Why should he get anything? That's *not* fair." The boy looked ready to cry.

"Oh, yes, it is," the teacher insisted. "Yes, it is. For the first time in your lives, you children are going to learn what it means to be fair. Now, everyone open your books!"

On Saturday morning Molly went to soccer practice. Thank goodness everything there was normal. The only unusual thing happened as practice was wrapping up. Molly was changing her shoes when she looked across the Academy wall and saw someone in The Hedges.

The Hedges were a long row of bushes on the north side of town. They were high shrubs that had been there forever and were so wild that no one ever bothered to tear them down. They were the unofficial border of Laurentide since beyond them was nothing but the gloomy forest that stretched over the hills to Pug.

"Did you see that?" Molly asked the girl next to her.

"See what?"

"I saw someone in the Hedges. Someone...there! Look over there."

They stood on a bench and looked across the wall. There *was* someone in the Hedges. Short, squat, with unusually long arms and long hair, the person pulled back into the bushes when he saw them looking his way.

"What was that?" the other girl asked.

"I don't know," Molly admitted. They told their coach but he decided they must have seen an animal. He told them to forget about it.

"Your father called while you were at practice," Aunt Marcy told her at lunch.

"He did?!" Molly exclaimed. "Is he coming home?"

"Not until next Saturday. But that's two days early," Aunt Marcy added when Molly slumped back into her seat.

"Yes, it's two days early," Molly grumbled. "But it's still two days late. My history test is on Thursday."

"Haven't you been studying?"

"Yes, but there's a lot to know," Molly insisted. "It's an American history test, everything from the Constitution to the Second World War, whenever that was. I didn't even know we had a *First* World War."

"Well, of course we had a First World War," said Aunt Marcy. "Don't be silly."

"When?" Molly asked.

"Well, um..." Aunt Marcy said, thinking. "I'm not sure but it was probably before the Second World War, of course."

"Uh-huh. Thanks. I wish Mom had taken me to Chicago with her."

"You would have missed too much school," Aunt Marcy reminded her. "And besides, she's just helping your grandparents with their spring cleaning. You wouldn't want to wash windows and rake the yard all day, would you?"

"No, but maybe we would have had time to go to the Museum."

"Which museum?"

"Which museum? The Museum of Science and Industry, of course. It's only the best museum in the whole world. It's huge and awesome and has stuff you never see anywhere else."

"Well, maybe next time you're in Chicago you can go there," Aunt Marcy said, patting her hand.

"Yeah, next time." For some reason Molly found that phrase depressing. *Next time.* It made her feel like she had missed something. She had a sudden fear that Chicago would not be the same when she saw it again. "Well," she sighed, not knowing what else to do, "I guess I'll go practice the piano for a while. After that, if it's alright I want to run down to Dumfrey's Pet Shop."

"Oh?" said Aunt Marcy. "Are your parents getting a dog?"

"No. I just have some business to settle."

Dumfrey's Pet Shop was on Early Street, almost at the river. Molly rode her bike there late in the afternoon and went past the train station on the way. She shouldn't have since the station was so empty and depressing. The boarded up windows, the lonely old train car, and messy pigeons seemed to chase people away.

But then Town Square wasn't much busier. Even though it was a beautiful day few people were about. The Springer Candy Store was closed. The Haizlip car dealership was quiet, too. The only people in sight were a couple lounging outside Mr. Ashburn's restaurant, The Blind Pig. Molly rode past them to the shop with the green sign showing a laughing dog.

"Where is everybody?" she asked, going through the door. Peter Dumfrey was there alone, sweeping up spilled cat food.

"Is that your way of saying hello?" he asked.

"Hello," Molly said. "Where is everybody?"

"Probably at the meeting," he replied.

"What meeting?"

"Did you come here just to ask questions?" Peter asked. "Don't you want to buy something?"

"No," she told him. "What I really want is to tear your fingers off and feed them to that gerbil over there."

"Gerbils won't eat fingers," Peter laughed. "And why are you always talking about tearing off my arms and legs and fingers? That's not nice."

"You're one to talk! Why are you always putting animals in my backpack and scaring me out of my wits?"

"Because it's funny."

Molly grabbed a metal pooper-scooper. "You know what would be funny?" she asked. "Beating you over the head with this would be funny!"

"Hey, no," Peter said. "Put that down." He dropped his broom and fled down the aisle. Molly chased him through the shop until finally she trapped him in a corner where large white rabbits wandered inside a miniature town. Peter hopped behind the rabbit fence and hid. Molly swung her pooper-scooper at him.

"Come out of there, Peter," she threatened. "Come out so I can beat you over the head."

"Hey, be nice. I'm a hard-working salesman – we need encouragement, not threats."

"Are you afraid of a girl?"

"Yes – when they swing pooper-scoopers."

"I wouldn't if you weren't such a jerk."

"You should be grateful," he protested. "Not everyone gets a tree frog for a gift."

"A gift? You call sticking a frog in my pocket a gift?" Molly lowered the pooper-scooper. "Which reminds me: how did you get that thing in my pocket?"

"Oh, that was easy. I'll show you if you don't hit me."

Molly put away the scooper. "Okay," she gave in. Peter hopped out of the rabbit exhibit and grabbed a small rubber dog bone from a dish by the cash register.

"It's called sleight of hand," he explained. "It's where you pretend to have nothing in your hand but you really do." He lay the bone in his hand and squeezed it but kept his fingers spread. "Then if you want to drop it into someone's pocket, all you have to do is get close to them, pass your hand near the pocket, and relax your hand. But it's good to distract them first." He looked suddenly toward the front door. "Hey, is that Kate?"

Molly turned to look. "Where?"

"My mistake, it wasn't her," Peter laughed. "Anyway," he continued, "that's all you do." He held up his hand – it was empty.

Molly felt her pocket. Darn it if the dog bone wasn't there.

"That's good," she admitted. "But how do you know how to do that? Are you learning to be a pickpocket?"

"Pickpockets take things out of pockets," Peter reminded her. "I only know how to put things in. It's a basic magic trick. My dad gave me a book about the most famous magician ever, Harry Houdini. It's awesome. You want to see it?"

"No," Molly said. "But speaking of your dad, where is he?"

"He's at the meeting. Lots of people are there."

"What meeting?"

"The meeting to decide what to do about the woman from Pug and Mayor Smolt. Mr. Holmes thinks they've broken the law. And he's certain they have violated the Academy Trust. He and

Doctor Shelburne are leading a group to have them both removed from the Board of Trustees."

"What is a trustee, anyway? Or a trust?" Molly asked.

"I don't know," admitted Peter. "You'll have to ask my dad. Or maybe the Van Helsings. That's where they're meeting tonight."

"The Van Helsings?" Molly repeated. "How do you know them? And why were you at their shop yesterday?"

"Who, me?" Peter said quickly. "I wasn't."

"You're a horrible liar, Peter Dumfrey," Molly said. "I saw you."

"Okay, okay. I'm helping Mr. Van Helsing fix up one of their antiques. It's an old railroad repair car – it looks like a car that you drive on the street but it drives on rails instead. The Van Helsings are really into trains for some reason and they want it to run again."

"So why is that a secret?"

"I don't know that it is," Peter said. "But there are strange enough things going on these days that I don't want people thinking I'm weird, too."

"You *are* weird. But you're right that there are strange things going on."

"Like what?"

Molly told him about her math quiz and the corn flakes at the store. Peter listened carefully.

"You say none of the adults at the store knew what corn flakes are?"

"Nobody," Molly confirmed.

The bell jingled on the door just then as Peter's father entered the shop. He was a thin man with a soft voice. Molly liked him because he always took the time to say hello to her, as he did now.

"It's always good to see you, Molly, but you should go home. Peter, let's clean the cages and close up for the night."

"Is everything alright, Mr. Dumfrey? Did the meeting go well?"

"We made progress," he said with a sigh. "Mr. Holmes has a plan. If everything works out, we can turn that horrible woman out of Laurentide before the end of the week."

"Is she really horrible?" Molly asked. "She looks angry all the time but I can't imagine why."

"She is, Molly," Mr. Dumfrey assured her. "Ursula Bamcroft has been angry since the day she was born. Angry at everyone who has something she doesn't. Angry at everyone who she doesn't control. She's the reason Pug is such an unpleasant place these days."

"Why, what does she do?"

"Ursula Bamcroft finds people who don't have something and stirs them up. It doesn't matter what they don't have: money, or an education, or a nice house, or something. She convinces them that the reason they don't have something is because someone else has cheated them. In other words, she stirs up fights. She divides people. If you and Peter were life-long friends, Ursula Bamcroft could show up and ten minutes later you two would hate each other."

"We hate each other now," Peter shrugged.

"Well, you know what I mean," his dad said. "There are some people who make life better and there are some who make life worse. Ursula Bamcroft is only happy when she is making life worse. We think she has been planning a takeover of Laurentide Academy for years. And she has convinced the mayor to help her. She just doesn't like it because it is such a success for our town. I think if we left it up to her she would utterly destroy the school."

"Really?!" Peter and Molly said together.

"Absolutely. She would do here what she did to Pug. It was a nice town until she showed up and talked everyone into hating everyone else. Soon people were fighting over everything. Businesses left and people lost their jobs. Nobody felt confident about the future anymore. Folks became scared and when people get scared they make bad decisions – one was to elect Ursula Bamcroft the mayor. She promised to fix everything but instead she spent all their money. She put the whole town in debt. When that happened, Pug died. Only the lazy people stayed behind."

"Is she going to do that here?"

"She'll try. But we're not giving up. You never give up fighting for things you believe in and people here believe in Laurentide."

"But can you really make her leave?"

"Well, we'll have to move fast. She and the mayor will try to appoint new members to the Board of Trustees and each appointment will make things harder for us. So we have to do something this week."

"Mr. Dumfrey, what's a trust?" Molly asked.

Mr. Dumfrey looked at her. "A trust? Why, it's just a set of rules that people agree to follow. And trustees are people who are supposed to enforce the rules. Think of it like a soccer game – you play soccer, right?"

"Yes."

"Well, a trust is the rules of the game. If everybody went out on the field and did whatever they wanted, the game would fall apart. If each coach called everything a goal, or put fifty players on the field instead of ten, or let the players run out of bounds, it would be chaos, right?"

"It sure would," Molly agreed.

"Well, that's why you have rules. The rules are a 'trust.' In other words, everyone *trusts* everyone else to follow the rules and not do things that are wrong. And the referee is the trustee, the person who makes sure people behave. Our problem now is that at the Academy, Ms. Bamcroft is ignoring the rules. And somehow she has made the other referees disappear. She wants to make the school fall apart just like an out-of-control soccer game."

"What can we do?" Molly asked. "Can we help?"

Mr. Dumfrey walked her to the door.

"No, Molly. This is adult business. We'll work things out. Soon you can go back to school without having to worry about ridiculous things like sharing your grades or losing your teachers."

Molly climbed back on her bike and rode toward home. But when she passed the train station something caught her eye that hadn't been there before. Someone had pinned a note by the ticket window. She pulled alongside the platform to read it.

Thursday next. Eight O'Clock. Be timely, the note said.

"Who is this for?" she asked aloud. "What's at eight o'clock?"

But there was no one to answer her. The pigeons in the gutter just cooed and bobbed their heads. With a shrug Molly left the paper where it was. The last she saw of the note it was still pinned to the wall, fluttering in the afternoon breeze.

CHAPTER 4

Burglars

"Up!" cried Kate. "Up, up, up!"

Molly sat on her horse Bristol and laughed. Kate always shouted during her riding lesson whenever it was time to practice jumps. Kate's horse was perfectly capable of clearing the jumps outside the Academy stables but Kate never believed he would. To encourage him she yelled directions. The riding instructor, Mrs. Newtown, thought shouting at your horse was unprofessional but Kate wouldn't stop.

"Good job, Kate!" Molly called as Kate cleared the first hurdle. Kate waved.

"Up, up, up!" she cried as her horse approached the next jump. Mrs. Newtown shook her head.

It was Sunday afternoon and a beautiful day. A breeze from the north brought a fresh smell from the forest and a not so fresh smell from the stables.

Kate finished her jumps and trotted up beside Molly. Together the two of them watched Maddie Taylor go through the course. Maddie was annoying because she never stopped spreading gossip but Molly admired the way she rode. Maddie had perfect posture in the saddle and never yelled at her horse.

"She's good," Kate sighed.

"She is," Molly agreed. "I wish I could look that comfortable in a jump. I always freeze up like a popsicle."

When Maddie finished she trotted over with a big smile. "That was fun!"

"You looked like a professional," Molly told her. "Like a real competitive rider. You could give us all lessons."

Maddie beamed. "Thanks! Really, it was nothing. Say, do you guys want to know what I heard about those new students and Oscar Peel in third period math? They challenged him to a fight for no reason and..."

"Oh, hang on," Molly interrupted. "I'd love to but it's my time to jump. Why don't you tell Kate?"

"Thanks a lot," Kate muttered as Molly trotted off.

Molly led Bristol to the center of the arena where Mrs. Newtown waited.

"Now Molly, I want to see you improve on the things we talked about last week," Mrs. Newtown said, tapping a riding crop against Molly's leg. "Relax, sit up straight, and keep your eyes forward. Don't watch Bristol, watch where he's going. Lead with your body, not the reins. Bristol will go where you tell him but you have to tell him with your body. Do you understand?"

"Lead with my body, not the reins," Molly repeated, but she was looking at the first jump as she spoke. It had red supports and a striped pole laid between them. There were hay bales beneath the pole. Molly was just like Kate in that she was never quite sure Bristol would clear the pole. Most of the time he looked half-asleep. She always imagined him crashing into the pole and herself tumbling out of the saddle. It wasn't a pleasant image so during jumps she usually closed her eyes.

"And don't close your eyes," Mrs. Newtown reminded her.

"Don't close my eyes," Molly repeated.

"And don't freeze up. You look like a popsicle."

But as she and Bristol walked, then trotted, then cantered around the arena and approached the first jump, Molly forgot everything Mrs. Newtown said. She froze, flopped forward, and closed her eyes.

"Jump," she whispered.

Bristol jumped but his rear hooves clipped the pole. Not enough to trip, just enough to rattle the pole in its clips and scare Molly half to death.

"You're okay, Molly!" she heard Kate call. "Just a little higher next time!"

"*Lean* forward," Mrs. Newtown yelled. "Don't crawl out on his neck. And keep your eyes open!"

Molly cantered Bristol in a circle while she calmed down. *Keep your eyes open*, she told herself. *And don't be a popsicle.*

The next two jumps went much the same way. Bristol cleared them but Molly didn't help. On the last jump she managed to keep her eyes open but she still slumped forward, practically lying flat on Bristol's neck.

"Good job," Maddie said generously as Molly trotted back to the waiting area.

Molly shook her head. "I get nervous," she explained. "I keep thinking about what might happen."

"That's your mistake," Maddie declared. "There are times when you should think and there are times when you should act. This is one of those times when you just act."

"Or maybe you should yell 'Up' more often," Kate suggested.

Mrs. Newtown gathered all the riders and opened the gates of the corral. "Time to let the horses cool down," she told them. "Take the Perimeter Trail, everyone. Just a quiet ride – no galloping and stay off the grass. Be back in twenty minutes."

The Perimeter Trail looped inside the Academy walls. Outside the walls was forest. Inside were the great lawns and stately trees of the Academy grounds. The Academy itself rose over it all with a silent dignity. Its wide doors and brick walls seemed especially quiet on a Sunday.

"So what did Maddie tell you?" Molly asked Kate as they rode along at the back of the group of riders.

"Nothing much. She says the new students are all bullies. Two of them challenged Oscar to a fight simply because he wouldn't tell them the answers to a quiz."

"What did he do?"

"He reported them but the teacher told him not to be a crybaby. Have you ever heard of such a thing?"

"Not at Laurentide," Molly admitted. "But there are a lot of things happening that we've never seen before."

"Anyway, I guess they tried to beat him up but were chased away by Bair Burton."

"Bair?" Molly asked. "The big guy whose mouth is always open? Why would he help Oscar?"

"Bair's a nice guy."

"He seems kind of dumb to me."

Kate frowned at Molly. "Don't say that. Bair's not dumb. He just thinks slow. Now, his little brother Stout is the one I'm not sure about. All Stout ever talks about is football."

"How do you know so much?" Molly demanded. "First I learn that you're passing information to Peter Dumfrey, now it seems you're friends with Bair and Stout?"

"We have, um, similar interests," Kate said carefully.

Molly was going to reply but over Kate's shoulder she saw movement in one of the Academy windows.

"Hey, someone's inside," she said.

"Inside where?"

"Inside the school. I just saw someone. Isn't that the lab?"

Other students heard her and stopped their horses. They had reached the back of the Academy estate.

"There," a girl pointed. "By the sundial. That door is open. And look! There's a broken window."

There was a door below Students Hall where teachers could enter. It opened onto a gravel driveway that surrounded the Academy like a ring. Picnic tables and a sundial sat next to the path. Normally on a weekend the door would be locked but today it was wide open.

"Someone tell Mrs. Newtown," Maddie suggested. Nobody moved at first but then Molly started to walk Bristol up the lawn toward the building.

"Molly, where are you going?" Kate whispered.

"To see who has broken into my school!" Molly replied angrily.

Kate and a few students followed Molly. Two others raced off to tell Mrs. Newtown about the break-in. The rest waited on the trail.

"We're not supposed to ride on the lawn," Kate reminded them as they trotted their horses up to the Academy. The horses seemed to agree with her. They stepped lightly across the grass as though afraid someone might see them, occasionally throwing up clods of dirt where their hooves dug in.

"I know," said Molly. "But isn't it so much softer than the trail?"

The faculty door was open. That didn't shock the students as much as seeing what someone had used to prop the door in place.

"Oh, my gosh!" said Kate. "It's one of the Memorial Cups from Students Hall!"

The door was held open by one of the polished silver cups that normally sat high on the wall by the student portraits. It was jammed into the gravel like a common doorstop.

One of the boys climbed down from his horse and pulled the cup out of the dirt. When he did the door swung closed with a *bang*. Seconds later there was a crash inside the building and the sound of panicked movement.

"Over there," the boy pointed. "The noise came from that classroom."

Molly turned Bristol in the direction of the sound. The other students followed. Together they rode up and down the back of the building, peering in windows.

"There!" cried a girl. "I saw somebody in my arts room."

"And somebody's running through the lab!" Kate called.

"I think they're trying to get out," the boy with the cup yelled back. "They know we're out here."

"Everyone!" Molly shouted. "Stick together."

She sounded so sure of herself that the other students immediately followed her instructions. But just as the riders came together there was a horrible screech from inside the building. At the same time a chair came flying through a window. Glass flew in all directions, startling the students and causing the horses to rear.

"Back up!" Molly urged the others. "Back up onto the grass!"

Before anyone could move a dozen figures leaped through the window, surprising them all.

The thieves were short, no bigger than Molly herself, but they were the oddest-looking people she had ever seen. They wore long waistcoats, shorts, and floppy hats. Some had sashes across their middle like wild gypsies. Some had bare feet while others wore boots. All had really long hair and long arms.

One after another the thieves leaped out and crashed onto the gravel, screaming at the top of their lungs. Then quick as a flash they were up and running across the lawn. Their sudden appearance scared the horses so much the students had their hands full staying in their saddles. But that wasn't the worst of it.

A final figure leaped through the window. He was short and stout and his arms hung almost to the gravel. His hair was as long as his arms and he even had little tufts that stuck out on his face. His nose was wide and his eyebrows thick and bushy. A red sash tied a moth-eaten coat around his waist. He was the ugliest person Molly had ever seen. Before she could say anything the thief opened his mouth and let loose a screech that was so loud it should have broken all the windows in the Academy.

The horses freaked out. Two of the students were thrown. Kate jumped free of her saddle as her horse reared high. The others galloped off in terror.

Molly was scared, too, but when Bristol reared up she reacted without thinking. She dug one heel into his side and hauled sharply on the reins to bring him into a tight turn. Instead of toppling backward Bristol spun and backed up behind the picnic tables. There he found himself trapped. When he realized he had nowhere to go he stopped struggling. That gave Molly a chance to look around.

What she saw was chaos. The school alarm was going off, glass was everywhere, horses were running free, and Kate lay on the grass. Most of the burglars, fast as greyhounds, had run all the way to the wall and were climbing over it to disappear into the forest. But the last one was still racing across the lawn, carrying a bag packed with silver Memorial Cups. Deep inside Molly felt a wave of anger build.

"Oh, no you don't," she growled. "You DO NOT steal from my school. Come on, Bristol. Up, up, up!"

With an explosion of energy Bristol leaped over the picnic tables and burst into a run.

"Molly!" Kate yelled. "Come back! Wait for help!"

I'll wait for help, Molly thought as Bristol galloped over the grass. I'll wait while Bristol is stomping all over that fat gypsy's head...

Bristol was a thoroughbred and born to run. He and Molly rapidly closed the distance on the burglar. When the gypsy looked over his shoulder and saw her coming he realized he couldn't get away in a straight line so he swiftly cut to his right into the flower-erbeds by the pond. Molly leaned right to cut him off. Bristol turned and caught up with the man before he got to the water. But the burglar then cut left and with a leap that Molly didn't think possible he jumped across the whole pond. He and Molly were now on opposite sides of the water!

Molly spurred Bristol onward. Together they raced down one side of the pond while the burglar ran down the other, seeing who could reach the perimeter wall first. At the end of the water she leaned left: Bristol turned and without breaking stride leaped over a picket fence that bordered the pond at that end. Coming down he almost landed on the gypsy, who shrieked in terror and leaped away. But Molly had her riding crop out. As Bristol passed she swung it and smacked the burglar sharply on the side of the head.

"Aaiieeee!!"

The burglar yelled and dropped his bag. Silver cups spilled everywhere. He stopped to collect them but Molly now leaned back in the saddle and squeezed her legs: Bristol slid to a halt, tearing up great clumps of turf. He spun around and charged back toward the burglar who gave up all thought of the silver and made a bee-line straight for the Academy wall. This time he ran as though his pants were on fire.

If the wall had been a little farther away Molly and Bristol would have caught the thief. But with his headstart the gypsy got there first. He leaped to the top of the wall in a single jump, just avoiding Bristol's hooves. The odd-looking man screamed one more time and then vanished into the forest.

Molly waved her crop as Bristol stomped his feet.

"And don't come back!" she yelled.

The Academy grounds fell quiet again. Molly's heart raced. She felt a sudden need to lie down. Dropping from the saddle, she lay on the grass and waited for the butterflies in her stomach to settle down. Bristol stood beside her.

Mrs. Newtown and Maddie galloped up followed by the other students.

"Molly! Molly! Are you hurt?" Mrs. Newtown called.

"I'm okay," Molly answered. "I'm just waiting for my legs to stop shaking."

"That was amazing, Molly!" Maddie exclaimed. "I can't believe what I just saw – that was the best riding ever! You were going a million miles an hour and you jumped that fence like it was nothing. You should be giving *me* lessons!"

"Ohhhh," Molly groaned. Even lying on the ground she still felt as if they were galloping at top speed. She looked over to see if Bristol was also trembling but he wasn't. In fact he looked as sleepy as ever, chewing grass and swishing his tail. He even returned her gaze with an expression that said, *Don't mention it. It was nothing.*

CHAPTER 5

The Troublemaker

MOLLY DIDN'T KNOW what to expect when she went to school on Monday. Laurentide Academy was abuzz with rumors. Every student had questions. Molly kept quiet and told everyone who asked to talk to Kate instead.

So when she was called to the Headmaster's office after lunch she assumed it was because Ms. Bamcroft had questions, too. But she was wrong.

"Aunt Marcy, what are you doing here?"

Aunt Marcy stood in the Headmaster's office holding Michael in her arms. Before she could answer, another voice spoke for her.

"She's here because I told her to be here," the voice said.

The voice belonged to Ursula Bamcroft.

"You are in deep trouble, missy," Ms. Bamcroft continued. She sat behind a desk and squinted through eyes that were heavy with mascara.

"I'm not Missy, I'm Molly," Molly replied.

"Don't be cute with me!" Ms. Bamcroft snapped. "What in the world were you doing yesterday, galloping around the Academy, breaking windows, tearing up the grass, and putting the very school in danger? The police have been here all morning."

Molly didn't know how to answer. She looked up at Aunt Marcy who as usual tried to calm things down.

"I believe there has been a misunderstanding..." Aunt Marcy started to say but Ursula Bamcroft cut her off.

"Were you there?" she demanded. "I didn't think so. So you don't know what happened any more than anyone else."

"No, but Molly told me everything," Aunt Marcy said. "She said that..."

"'*Molly said?*' '*Molly said?*'" Ms. Bamcroft mocked. "It seems to me Molly has created quite a tale of events. Well, I've had the police in here and what they tell me they found when they arrived yesterday was a bunch of students – led by Little Missy here – running loose on the grounds. Broken windows, broken doors, and horses tearing up the grounds. Oh, and did I mention a sack full of silver cups, stolen right from Students Hall?"

"That's right," Molly interrupted. "That's why we called the police. Those gypsies broke in and stole the cups."

"Gypsies?" Ms. Bamcroft sneered. "Oh, yes. I forgot the little story she made up about gypsies."

"I didn't make it up," Molly insisted. "There were these men in funny clothing and..."

"Do you know the first thing about gypsies?" Ms. Bamcroft demanded.

"What?"

"Why are you blaming gypsies, a poor group of oppressed people who only want to sing and dance?"

"Uh, well I don't know that they were actual gypsies," Molly stuttered. "I just said gypsies because they were dressed in all kinds of clothing and looked kind of wild..."

"What a horrible thing to say! So you're a hater as well as a thief?"

"What? I'm not either. Someone broke into our school and I tried to stop them."

"She did a brave thing," Aunt Marcy added. "Foolish but brave. She should have reported it immediately to Mrs. Newtown and let her handle it."

"We did report it," Molly explained. "But when I saw the broken window I got upset. I wanted to see who was in our school."

"'*Our school*,' '*our school*,'" Ms Bamcroft mimicked. "You talk as though you own this place. Laurentide Academy doesn't belong to you, missy. It belongs to the people."

"What people?" Molly asked.

"Don't backtalk me! All the people. It's owned by everybody."

"Actually," Aunt Marcy said, "Laurentide is a private school. It was founded by Lady Elizabeth Shelbourne in 1869 with the fortune she inherited from her father. It belongs to the town which is why you have to live here to attend the school."

Ursula Bamcroft scowled. She came out from behind her desk and stood close to Molly and her aunt so she could glare down at them. Her pantsuit smelled like old hay.

"Isn't that nice? Some rich girl leaves a bunch of money to you so that makes you better than anyone else?"

"It doesn't have anything to do with being better. It has to do with the Trust she left..."

"So you admit it!" Ms. Bamcroft exclaimed. "You think you're better! Well, did it ever occur to you that little Lady Shelbourne didn't build this Academy all by herself? *She* didn't build it at all. Other people built it. Workers like bricklayers and carpenters and gardeners built it. Somebody else built that road you drive on to get here. Somebody else invented the electricity that turns these lights on. The government has kept you safe here all these years so you can go to class and ride your precious horses. In other words, that little Lady Spoiled Brat didn't build this place. The government and those working people own this school just as much as you do."

D. M. Sears

Molly was completely lost. "What are we even talking about?" she asked Aunt Marcy, who could barely speak she was so astonished. "Are the police going to catch the gypsies...I mean, the burglars?" she corrected herself.

Ursula Bamcroft scowled again.

"There were no gypsies," she declared.

"What?!"

"I don't believe a word of your story. You and your friends broke into the school."

"That's not true!" Molly cried.

"Now you wait just a minute," Aunt Marcy demanded. "Molly is as honest as the day is long and..."

"Oh, blah, blah, blah," Ms. Bamcroft interrupted. "You don't know if she's telling the truth any more than I do. You're not even her mother."

"Why, I have never heard such talk in all my life," Aunt Marcy gasped. "Who are you to say such a thing? You don't know the first thing about me or Molly – or Laurentide Academy, for that matter – and now you're talking nonsense. If Molly says gypsies broke into the school then that's exactly what happened and you had better do something about it!"

The scowl didn't budge. "What I'm going to do is put your niece on probation," Ursula said.

"Why me?"

"Because I can't prove you broke into the school but even if you didn't you could have caused all kinds of trouble with your little stunts. What if you had hurt yourself? Lawsuits, that's what you would have filed! Lawsuits blaming everyone for you getting hurt. You probably want some of that wonderful Shelbourne fortune. Well, we'll share all that wealth but that's not the way we're going to do it."

"That is the most preposterous thing I've ever heard," Aunt Marcy replied.

"It certainly is," Molly protested. "Mr. Gladden would never have suggested anything like that about me."

"Who's Mr. Gladden?" her aunt asked.

"What do you mean, who's Mr. Gladden?" Molly said, surprised. "The Headmaster! I mean, the Headmaster before...her." She pointed to Ursula Bamcroft.

"Oh, that's right," Aunt Marcy remembered. "How silly of me. I forgot."

Ms. Bamcroft laughed. "Yes, you forgot. That old fool Gladden isn't here anymore," she cackled. "And soon you'll forget all about him. I'm the Headmaster now and you had better get used to it. And everyone is going to be equal, I'll make sure of that. Equal and fair. Now get out of here. And Molly," she added as Molly hurried to leave, "I'm watching you from now on. You're a troublemaker. One false step and you'll be gone from Laurentide Academy forever."

Molly was so upset that Aunt Marcy didn't let her return to class that day. Instead she went home and straight up to her room where she cried until she couldn't cry anymore. A trouble-maker? Nobody had ever called her a troublemaker in her life. And Ms. Bamcroft threatened to throw her out of Laurentide Academy! Molly couldn't imagine such a disaster. Laurentide was her life. Her friends were there, her teachers were there – at least the ones who hadn't been fired in the last week. Her horse Bristol was there. She couldn't imagine being anywhere else. But at the same time she couldn't imagine being there so long as Ursula Bamcroft was the Headmaster. Even if nothing like the burglary ever happened again, Molly could imagine Ursula thinking up some other excuse to expel her from the Academy. Just the thought made Molly cry until she fell asleep.

"Molly, I have to talk to you," Peter said the next day.

"Not now, Peter."

"It's important," Peter insisted. "I want you to come with me somewhere after school."

"Eww, please, Peter! I don't want to go out with you!"

"What?" Peter stopped. "I just want you to meet someone."

"Peter, I'm not in a good mood, okay? My whole world is falling apart. I don't want to meet any of your friends."

"It's not one of my friends. Well, sort of...but..."

"No," Molly cut him off, and slipped into her math class.

At lunch Molly grabbed Kate and the two of them hurried outside. Molly couldn't help crying again as she told her friend everything that had happened in the Headmaster's office.

"She said all those things?" Kate gasped.

"And more," Molly sobbed. "She doesn't believe our story. She thinks we broke in."

"I know. She told me the same thing."

"She did? Did you get yelled at, too?"

"No," Kate told her. "Actually, when I was called to the office she was all nice and friendly – it was creepy."

"What?" Molly demanded. "What did she say?"

"She said it was still unclear what happened on Sunday," Kate remembered. "That the police were investigating but that it might all have been a misunderstanding."

"A misunderstanding about what? There were a bunch of weird guys stealing from the school. What is there to misunderstand?"

"I don't know," Kate said, and she lowered her voice to a whisper. "But she was trying to get me to say that you had started it, Molly."

"What?!"

Kate nodded.

"Why?" Molly said. "Why does she hate me?"

"I don't know," Kate answered. "But you want to hear something even weirder? I talked to Maddie and she said Ms. Bamcroft did the same thing with her. Except get this...with her, Ms. Bamcroft was trying to get Maddie to blame it all on you *and* me!"

Molly's mouth hung open in disbelief. Then she remembered what Mr. Dumfrey had said at the pet shop.

"She's trying to divide us," she said.

"What?"

"Peter's dad said he knew all about people like Ms. Bamcroft. He said she would try to divide us, try to get us all to hate each other. That's how she gets what she wants."

"But what does she want?" Kate asked.

"She wants to destroy Laurentide," a voice behind them said.

The two girls jumped. It was Peter Dumfrey.

"Peter, don't creep up on people!"

"I didn't. You guys just aren't paying attention."

"How do you know Ms. Bamcroft wants to destroy Laurentide?" Kate demanded. "Why would she do that? She just became the Headmaster."

"She doesn't care about being Headmaster," Peter said, sitting on a bench by one of the flowerbeds. "She only became Headmaster so she could figure out a way to make the school and the town fall apart. That's what she's doing. And she has help."

"How do you know?" Molly asked.

"My dad told me," Peter replied.

"Does he have a plan to stop her?"

"Do *they* have a plan, you mean," Peter corrected her. "It's all the adults, remember? No, I don't think they have a plan yet but they're working on it. And they'll have to hurry."

"Why?"

"Because somebody found out about their meetings."

"The gypsies, I bet," Molly said.

"They aren't gypsies," Peter corrected her. "And now they're trying to scare my dad away. This morning someone threw a brick through our store window."

"What?!"

Peter nodded glumly. "Yup. Not just a brick, either. A wad of burning rags. My dad showed up just in time to put the fire out. Nothing like that has ever happened."

"They tried to burn down the pet store?" gasped Kate. "With the animals inside?"

"Yes."

"I want to go home," Molly said nervously. "I want to go home and stay there until my mom and dad are back."

"Maybe by then Mr. Holmes will have taken care of Ms. Bamcroft," said Peter. "But Molly, just in case his plan doesn't work I want you to come with me after school."

"There you go again with that, Peter. I'm not going out with your friends."

"Not friends, Molly. Just one friend. I want you to see Mrs. Van Helsing."

"From the antique store? Why?"

"Because she wants to see you."

"She doesn't even know me," Molly protested.

"But she's heard of you. I told her about the corn flakes and about you chasing the burglars."

"Corn flakes?" said Kate. "What are you talking about?"

"There are no corn flakes in town," Molly explained.

"None," Peter agreed. "Hershey bars are missing, too."

"So?" Kate demanded. "How is that important?"

"It's very important," Peter insisted. "I told Mrs. Van Helsing and she asked to meet Molly as soon as possible."

"I'm confused," Kate complained.

"Me, too," Molly said. She was afraid all of a sudden and didn't know why. "I don't know what any of this has to do with me."

The bell rang to announce the end of lunch period.

"Come with me after school," Peter pleaded. "Please, just talk to Mrs. Van Helsing. She'll know what to do."

CHAPTER 6

Mrs. Van Helsing

Mrs. Isabelle Van Helsing was not well. She sat inside the antique shop away from the windows with a blanket over her lap. Her breathing was raspy. Her eyes watered.

"Are you sick?" Molly asked, which was not a polite question but she couldn't help herself.

Mrs. Van Helsing touched a handkerchief to her eyes.

"Ah, Molly," she said. "Peter said you were direct. Sit down, please."

There weren't many places to sit, the shop was so stuffed with junk. There were old statues and desks and floor lamps everywhere. There were model cars and trains on shelves, dusty paintings on the walls, and old-fashioned jewelry stacked on the counter. A child's wagon from the 1920s sat in a corner next to a box of stuffed toys. Above the toys was a crate full of teacups, and above that model airplanes hung on string from the ceiling. There were grandfather clocks and wash tubs and butter churns and an old ice box that looked as solid as a bank safe. The store was so full there was no room to turn around. There were even antiques in the yard: through the back door Molly saw the old railroad repair car that Mr. Van Helsing was putting back together. It looked like a pickup truck but had train wheels instead of tires.

If there was any order to the shop Molly couldn't see it. The only spot that was tidy was a display case where Mr. Van Helsing kept his collection of Civil War photographs.

She settled onto a milking stool while Peter found a barber's chair from the early 1900s.

"I'm not sick," Mrs. Van Helsing continued. "But I've been hurt. It's difficult for me to breathe and my eyes don't like bright light anymore."

The three of them sat for a minute. The grandfather clocks ticked all around.

"Peter said you wanted to see me," Molly said finally. "Um, how do you two know each other?"

"Oh, Peter is my savior," Mrs. Van Helsing said. "I don't get around much so Peter helps me know what's going on. He told me about your encounter with the Pug-Nasties."

"With the what?"

"The Pug-Nasties," Peter repeated. "I told you they weren't gypsies."

"What's a Pug-Nasty?" Molly asked. "It sounds like a bug."

"It's not a bug, unfortunately," Mrs. Van Helsing lamented. "If they were bugs we could call an exterminator. But it's not that easy."

"They come from Pug," Peter continued. "Ms. Bamcroft uses them to create trouble."

"They're people from Pug?" Molly tried to understand. "They don't look like people. They look like the Seven Dwarves except with really old clothes."

"They're not dwarves," Mrs. Van Helsing corrected her. "They're not people at all. Well, once upon a time they were but traveling without a ticket twisted them into foul little creatures who make nothing but mischief."

"Doing what?"

Mrs. Van Helsing looked at Peter. "You haven't told her?" she asked.

Peter shook his head.

Mrs. Van Helsing sighed. "It sounds like we'll have to back up a little. Molly, tell me something: what do you think of Ursula Bamcroft?"

Molly shivered. "I think she's very unpleasant," she said. "I never knew one person could cause so much trouble. She wants to force everyone to do what she wants."

"What do you mean?"

"She has weird ideas," Molly shrugged. "As though she doesn't understand how people really think. She keeps talking about fairness but then she does things that are unfair, like mixing up grades and letting anyone into Laurentide. Yesterday she told the soccer team that we have to let everyone join even if they can't run, and this morning I couldn't go to my art class because it was full of students from Pug. Ms. Bamcroft said last week if we liked our classes we could keep them, and if we liked our teachers we could keep them. But none of that is true. She's cancelling classes and firing teachers and everyone seems to be too afraid to stop her. Anyone who complains is called a hater. And she tells us that *we're* the ones being unfair."

"And you think that's odd?" Mrs. Van Helsing asked.

"Of course it's odd! And it's wrong. It's like Ms. Bamcroft never grew up. Her life seems to be one long temper-tantrum."

Mrs. Van Helsing nodded. "It has certainly been long. You're perceptive, Molly. You notice things. I hear you have something to tell me about corn flakes." She pointed to a picture on the wall above the jewelry counter. It was an old, old advertisement for

Kellogg's Corn Flakes that showed a smiling woman holding a cornstalk. The ad read: "The Sweetheart Of The Corn."

"Yes," Molly replied. "There aren't any. Not anymore. I've looked in all the stores and they're gone. And nobody seems to remember them."

"Who doesn't remember them?"

"The people in the store. And my Aunt Marcy."

"Adults?"

"Yes," Molly replied.

"Of course," Mrs. Van Helsing said. "Adults always forget first."

"And Hershey bars," Peter added. "They're missing, too."

The door opened and Mr. Van Helsing came in.

"Hello, my love," he greeted his wife. "Hello, Peter. And hello..."

Molly introduced herself.

"Hello, Molly." Mr. Van Helsing kissed his wife and looked around for a place to sit. Not finding one, he leaned on an old soda machine. "Are we having a meeting?"

"Molly is the young lady who chased the Pug-Nasties out of the Academy," Mrs. Van Helsing explained.

"It was brave of you, Molly, to go after the Pug-Nasties," Mr. Van Helsing said. "I'm glad you weren't hurt."

"We were just discussing Ursula Bamcroft," Mrs. Van Helsing added. "Where she comes from and why she causes so much trouble."

"Ah, yes. And that trouble is getting worse. Some people in town are forgetting."

"So Molly was saying," his wife told him. "What have you heard?"

"Well, we had a meeting just now about the Trustees and some of them couldn't remember the Haizlips."

"The Haizlips?" Peter asked. "How can anyone forget them? They have all those TV commercials for their car dealerships. Besides, Jennie is the star of the soccer team."

"I know. But people are forgetting and the commercials haven't been on TV since the whole Haizlip family disappeared."

"The mayor said they went on a vacation," Molly remembered.

Mr. Van Helsing shook his head. "If they did, no one can find them. And the other Trustees, too, are disappearing one by one. Old Charlie Ashburn has never taken a vacation but when I went to the Blind Pig this afternoon his manager said they hadn't seen him since the weekend."

"That is odd," Mrs. Van Helsing said softly. "Charles Ashburn started that restaurant fifty years ago after he moved here from Kansas City. It's his whole life."

Molly thought for a moment. "There's something else," she remembered. "Yesterday I had to remind my Aunt Marcy about Mr. Gladden. Normally Aunt Marcy never forgets a face."

Mrs. Van Helsing looked at her husband with concern.

"Are you thinking what I'm thinking?" she asked.

"I think someone has done something un-historical," he replied. "Someone is blanking the Trustees in order to make room for Ursula and her cronies."

"What's blanking?" Peter asked.

"It's the most horrible thing that can happen to a person," Mr. Van Helsing replied. "It's when someone intercepts your history and changes it. Changes it so you never exist."

Molly and Peter looked at each other. "Why would anyone do that?" Molly asked. "And how?"

"Well," Mrs. Van Helsing said in her soft voice. "I'll tell you a story. Maybe it will help you understand. Once upon a time, a girl grew up in England. Her father was a lord so the girl of course was a lady. Lady Elizabeth."

"You're talking about Lady Shelbourne," Molly guessed.

"Yes," Mrs. Van Helsing nodded. "Lady Elizabeth Shelbourne. Her father was wealthy but he earned his money. He worked in the coal business and later was one of the first people to build railroads. He became very rich. But even before that Lady Elizabeth noticed there was something strange about the schools she attended and the friends she had. Everyone she spent time with was also a member of the aristocracy."

"What's an aristocracy?" Peter asked.

"An aristocracy," Mr. Van Helsing explained, "is when a group of people put themselves higher than everyone else in a society."

"Rich people?"

"No," said Mr. Van Helsing. "Anyone can become rich by working hard and saving their money. To be a member of the aristocracy you have to be born into the right family."

"But nobody can control which family they're born into," Peter pointed out.

"Exactly," said Mrs. Van Helsing. "That's what bothered Elizabeth Shelbourne. She noticed that only members of the right families could get into her school. Even if they weren't that smart or if they were lazy and didn't want to study, they could get in just because of their name. And because they went to the right schools and were from the right families, they ended up growing up and being in charge of things and in powerful positions in the world."

"And she didn't like that?" Molly asked.

"She didn't think it was right," Mrs. Van Helsing said. "She thought if you were smart and worked hard that you should have a chance to go to a good school. So when her father left her an inheritance, she decided to take the money and start a school where anyone could attend if they could pass an entrance exam and promised to work hard."

"And that was Laurentide Academy!" Peter announced.

"No," Mrs. Van Helsing corrected him. "Actually it wasn't. Lady Shelbourne opened a school in England first – but it didn't work. This was in the 1800s. In England at that time everything depended on what family you were born into instead of what you yourself could do. So after failing to get a school going in England, Lady Shelbourne did what many people at that time were doing. She came to America, where people could get ahead just by working hard and where nobody cared what family you were from."

"That's why she came here?" Molly asked.

"That's why," Mrs. Van Helsing continued. "At first she thought she would open her school in one of the big cities like New York. But there she found people as stuffy as they were in England. So instead she got on a train and moved west. That's how she ended up in Ohio. This is where she found the small town of Laurentide and where she offered to build a school. She insisted on only two rules: one, that any student could attend so long as they agreed to study and work hard; and two, that students and teachers had to live in the town – because she wanted the school and the town to feel like they were part of the same family."

"But what does that have to do with Ms. Bamcroft?" Molly asked.

"Ursula Bamcroft grew up back east, in a family that had plenty of money. She had everything she wanted growing up. Her parents spoiled her with the most expensive clothes, the nicest toys, and the best schools. But then her father ran off and abandoned the family, and sometime later her mother left, too. Ursula was raised by her grandparents. They tried to raise her well – they even brought her to Laurentide and enrolled her in the Academy."

"They what?!" Peter and Molly cried in unison.

"That's right," Mr. Van Helsing said. "Ursula Bamcroft attended the Academy for a while. But she didn't stay long."

"Why not?"

"Let's just say she was not a good fit. After a year someone gave her a chance to move on and she took it. She never came back."

"I wonder if that was around the time my mom was a student," Molly said.

"Actually," chuckled Mr. Van Helsing. "Ursula Bamcroft is not as young as your mother. She's older than she looks."

"We can talk about that later," Mrs. Van Helsing interrupted him.

Molly was thinking. "So does that explain why Ms. Bamcroft hates the Academy? Is that why she hates me, because I'm here and she's not?"

"It's more than jealousy," Mrs. Van Helsing explained. "It's about control. Ursula Bamcroft wants power. She wants to tell people what to do. But we're not going to let her."

"Now Isabelle," her husband cautioned. "Don't get any ideas. You're not in any condition to confront Ursula Bamcroft."

"I will do what I must," Mrs. Van Helsing said firmly.

Mr. Van Helsing looked worried. "Yes, I suppose you will. You've done it before. But that reminds me of something I must do. I need to see Mr. Holmes." He kissed his wife on the forehead and headed for the door. As he passed the display case with his

Civil War photos, he gently arranged them even though they were already in perfect order.

"Will you be home for dinner?" Mrs. Van Helsing asked.

"Oh, certainly. I never miss dinner, do I?"

"No, you don't. You are very timely that way."

Mr. Van Helsing left.

"That's the second time this week I've heard that word," Molly remarked. "Timely. It's not one that most people use."

"Where else did you hear it?" Mrs. Van Helsing asked.

"Actually I read it. There was a note at the train station that said something about Thursday, and how someone had to be timely."

Mrs. Van Helsing almost fell out of her chair in shock. "What??" she cried. "What note? Where is it?" She looked at Peter but he was as surprised as she was.

"I didn't see it!" he insisted. "I've checked every day and it wasn't there."

Their reaction surprised Molly.

"I didn't take it," she explained. "I left it where it was."

"When did you find the note, Molly? Where is it?"

Molly told them how she had discovered the note pinned to the ticket window. "And it was still there when I rode away," she said. "That was Saturday at dinner time."

Peter was crestfallen. "I've checked every day, Mrs. Van Helsing. I promise. I looked Saturday morning and again on Sunday. There was nothing there."

"Was the note for you, Peter?" Molly asked.

"No." He pointed to Mrs. Van Helsing. "It was for her. I was supposed to bring it to her the instant it showed up. But I missed it."

Mrs. Van Helsing took Molly's hand. "Molly, what did the note say exactly?"

Molly thought hard. She could picture the neat handwriting. "It said, '*Thursday next. Eight o'clock. Be timely*,'" she remembered. "That's it. I remember because it sounded very formal."

"Thursday next," Mrs. Van Helsing repeated. "Oh, dear. That's only two days from now."

"What will happen on Thursday?" Molly asked.

Mrs. Van Helsing didn't answer. A tear trickled down her cheek.

"Peter," she said. "Over there. Please, open that chest. There is a bag inside. Get it for me, will you?"

Peter opened the lid on a crate that sat next to the grandfather clock. Inside were riding boots, a coat, two tins of soda crackers, and a beautiful doll with smooth skin and long hair. Under them he found an old brown satchel. There were burn marks on the leather as though it had fallen into a fire, but mostly it was soft and supple to the touch.

"That's it," Mrs. Van Helsing said happily. "My courier bag. I haven't held it in years. I should have thought to look earlier..."

She flipped the buckle on the bag and lifted the flap. At first it seemed there was nothing inside. Then she reached in and pulled out a small piece of paper.

"What is it?" Peter asked. "Another note?"

"It's a ticket," Mrs. Van Helsing said quietly. "A train ticket."

"But for where?" Molly asked. "We don't have a train in Laurentide."

Mrs. Van Helsing clutched the satchel. "Thursday," she murmured. "Two days from now. And someone else has seen the note. That must be the case because it is missing now. They will know.

They will know their time is about to run out. Which means they will act soon."

"Who are you talking about, Mrs. Van Helsing?" Peter asked.

"Whose time is about to run out?" Molly added.

Mrs. Van Helsing had a faraway look in her eyes. "Peter," she said suddenly, "You must find Mr. Van Helsing immediately. Tell him about the note. And tell him about Thursday evening. Most importantly tell him to warn Doctor Shelbourne."

"Why? Is Doctor Shelbourne in trouble?"

"The Laurentide Trust," Mrs. Van Helsing explained quickly, "says that a descendant of Lady Elizabeth Shelbourne must serve on the Board of Trustees at all times for the Academy to continue. Doctor Shelbourne and Alan Springer are the only two descendants left of Lady Shelbourne. But now Mr. Springer is missing. That means the mayor and Ms. Bamcroft must put Doctor Shelbourne on the Board unless something happens to him, too. So he is in great danger."

Peter jumped up. "I'm on it," he said.

Mrs. Van Helsing grabbed his hand. "Be careful," she warned him. "Once you've seen Mr. Van Helsing, go right home and tell your father everything. I'm afraid Ursula Bamcroft will do something desperate."

"Why?"

"Because someone is coming who can stop her evil plans."

"I'll go," Peter promised. "Come on, Molly."

But before Molly could move Mrs. Van Helsing put a hand on her knee. "No, Peter. You go. Molly and I have things to talk about."

Peter dashed out the door and raced away. Behind him in the living room Mrs. Van Helsing and Molly huddled in conversation, the ticket for Thursday lying on the table between them.

CHAPTER 7

War

MOLLY WALKED OUT her front door on Wednesday and was struck on the head by a newspaper. It smelled like onions.

"Sorry!" came a call from the street. It was Devon Walters, the neighborhood paper boy. Devon ate so many onions that he smelled like one. He was pedaling by on his bicycle but screeched to a halt to apologize.

"Devon, aren't you late?" Molly asked. "You should be done with your route by now."

"I know," Devon panted, catching his breath. "I'm *wayyyy* late. But the drivers at the plant are on strike so everybody is behind schedule. And most of the delivery boys quit because of the change in their pay."

"Strike?" asked Molly. "Quit? Why?"

"Don't you read the news?" Devon asked. "Some guys from Pug stirred up all the workers at the plant. Everybody used to be happy but now half the plant is angry at the other half and they're all arguing over money. And now every delivery boy gets paid the same no matter how much we work. If I deliver to a hundred houses and another boy only delivers to two houses, we get the same pay. It's crazy. All the good workers are quitting. I'm going to quit as soon as I finish today's route."

"That is crazy," Molly thought as Devon sped away. But it wasn't as crazy as the headline on the newspaper that she picked up.

LAURENTIDE ACADEMY ERUPTS IN CIVIL WAR, the headline screamed.

"Citizens Group Brings Lawsuit Against Mayor and New Headmaster," Molly read. The article went on to explain how Dr. Shelbourne, Mr. Holmes, and Mr. Van Helsing were working to stop any changes to the Academy brought by Ms. Bamcroft.

"My poor little town," Molly groaned. "What has happened to it?"

At school Molly learned that two more of her teachers had been fired and replaced by substitutes from Pug. Poor Mrs. Julius, Molly's Latin teacher, even showed up to teach that morning but was told to go home. Ursula Bamcroft had decided that Latin was not important. Instead, the new substitute teacher announced that students would learn some language from Africa.

"Bantu?" Molly whispered to Kate. "What in the world is Bantu?"

Kate whispered back, "It sounds like a curse word."

The new teacher overheard her.

"That's a horrible thing to say!" she exclaimed. "Especially for you, Kate."

"Why me?" Kate asked.

"Because you're African-American," the teacher replied.

Molly looked at her friend. "You're African-American?" she asked.

Kate shrugged. "I don't think so. I've never been to Africa. We've always lived on Union Street."

"Really, Kate," the teacher snapped. "You should be on my side. Latin and all this stuff from America and Europe is just meant to keep you poor."

Kate laughed. "I'm not on anybody's side," she told the teacher. "And you must be confusing me with someone else. My mom's a foot doctor and my dad runs the Laurentide bank. We're not poor and we're not from Africa. We're American."

"*African*-American," the teacher corrected her.

"No," Kate said firmly. "*American.*"

"And I don't see why we should study some language nobody has ever heard of," another student spoke up. "Mrs. Julius said Latin is related to English and Spanish and Italian and French. What's Bantu related to?"

The new teacher wasn't sure. "It's um...uhh, well it's related to, uh..."

"I want to study Latin," Molly spoke up.

"Me, too," said Kate.

"Me, too," said several other students.

The teacher's face grew red. She grabbed a textbook and slapped it down on her desk.

"Be quiet!" she said. "Bantu is an important language and it will help you understand how people in Zimbabwe think."

"Where in the world is that?" said a student.

Everyone laughed except the teacher.

"Be quiet!" she yelled.

Peter caught up with Molly on her way home.

"I got the message to Mr. Van Helsing," he told her. "And Dr. Shelbourne. And guess what? They talked to the police and some judge – they're going to get Ms. Bamcroft fired! Maybe as early as tonight."

"Really? That's great, Peter. I don't know how much more of this we can take. The whole school is turning crazy."

"I know. I found out today Ms. Bamcroft won't let me work in the stables anymore. And my dad won't even leave his store now because he's afraid someone will attack it. I'm going to have to get a new job. I can't just sit around. And speaking of sitting, you were still sitting with Mrs. Van Helsing yesterday when I left. What did you two talk about?"

"Well," Molly said carefully. "Peter, I know she's a friend of yours but I think Mrs. Van Helsing is loony."

"She is not!"

"I'm sorry but she is. At first she wanted to talk to me about school, and soccer, and how I was doing in my classes, that kind of thing. She kept saying I reminded her of herself when she was twelve years old. But then she said she didn't think Mr. Holmes' plan would work, and how she had to catch a train on Thursday night, and how that was the only way to save Hershey bars, and how she was worried about Dr. Shelbourne disappearing."

"So?"

"So? What do you mean, so? She's going to save Hershey bars, Peter? From what? And how do you save a chocolate bar, anyway? Not to mention how is she going to get on a train when she can barely get out of her chair? Besides, nobody rides trains anymore. Oh, and did I mention the best part? Do you know where this magic train of hers is going, Peter?"

"Back in time," he answered.

Molly was shocked. "So you're loony, too?"

"I don't know if I am," Peter said. "But that's what Mr. and Mrs. Van Helsing told me. They asked us to keep it a secret."

"Us? Who's us?"

"The Guardian Team of Laurentide."

"The what?"

"The Guardian Team," he repeated. "Molly, I'm not the only one who helps Mrs. Van Helsing. She's trying to protect the Academy and people on the Guardian Team help her."

"Who else is on this so-called Guardian Team?" Molly asked. "I think you're making this up, Peter Dumfrey."

"I am not. Really, Molly," Peter insisted. "You have to believe me. There is a Guardian Team, and there is a train, and it's coming on Thursday with someone who can help Mrs. Van Helsing stop the destruction of Laurentide Academy. We just have to make sure Ms. Bamcroft doesn't do something horrible before the train gets here."

"Peter," Molly pleaded. "Trains don't come to Laurentide and they don't travel through time."

"Oh, really," he said. "Then how do you explain the Pug-Nasties? They don't look like anybody you've ever seen before, do they?"

"What does that have to do with trains? There are funny-looking people everywhere."

"Mrs. Van Helsing says the Pug-Nasties are friends of Ursula Bamcroft from over a hundred years ago. They were big bullies who used to attack factories and burn down businesses if they didn't get their way. Somehow Ms. Bamcroft snuck those bullies onto a train and brought them up to Pug to help her today. But she had a ticket and they didn't, and without a ticket they couldn't handle the time travel. It twisted them into Pug-Nasties."

Molly stared at Peter. "You're loonier than I thought," she said.

"I know, it sounds strange..."

"No, it's not strange, Peter. Strange is when you wear both socks on the same foot or eat ketchup on ice cream. Talking about time-traveling bullies is flat-out crazy. Wait a minute...did you say the Pug-Nasties are from a hundred years ago?"

"More than a hundred years," Peter confirmed. "I asked Mr. Van Helsing last night when Ursula Bamcroft attended Laurentide Academy and he said it was in 1892. So that means she's almost 140 years old."

Molly put her hands over her ears. "I am not listening to you! No, stop right there – don't follow me. I can't take this: my mom and dad are out of town, I have a history test to study for, and you're talking like somebody from the funny farm. Yes, that's right. You're crazy, the Van Helsings are crazy, and so is anyone who talks about a train or Pug-Nasties or traveling through time. Now leave me alone. I have to go study and try to remember who all the presidents were and why anyone cares. I certainly don't. Heck, I haven't even figured out when World War One happened. Good night!"

She turned and stomped up the sidewalk to her house. Peter called to her but she slammed the door in his face.

CHAPTER 8

The Fire

MOLLY WENT TO school on Thursday but at mid-morning a rumor raced through the classrooms that Ms. Bamcroft had been fired. No one knew if it was true but soon after they saw the new Headmaster run down the front steps and jump into her black car. She was mad enough to spit.

Then during lunch the teachers began to leave. The new ones, the ones Ursula Bamcroft had hired, walked away from their classrooms. By the time Molly arrived to her History class there was no one there to teach. Most students were packing up, too.

"What's going on?" she asked. "Where is everyone going?"

"School is closed," someone said. "The Headmaster left and so did the teachers."

"But we have class," Molly reminded them. "We have a test."

"So? If the teachers are gone, why should we stay?"

Because I studied and I want to take the test, Molly wanted to scream. But nobody was listening. Chaos, she remembered. That's what Mr. Dumfrey said Ursula Bamcroft would cause. Chaos.

She grabbed her backpack. She needed to find an adult. Students from every classroom were streaming toward the exit but Molly went down the hall the other way.

"Pssst! Molly! Over here."

"Maddie?"

Maddie was hiding behind the velvet drapes near the grand staircase.

"Maddie, what are you doing?"

"Shhh! Come here."

Molly stepped behind the drapes. Maddie pulled them shut.

"Maddie, why are you hiding? What's going on?"

"We have an assignment," Maddie whispered.

"A what?" Molly asked. "Who's we?"

But Maddie put a finger to her lips and signaled for Molly to wait. They stood listening for the sound of students to fade away. When it seemed that everyone was gone, Maddie peeked out and motioned for Molly to follow.

"What are we doing?" Molly whispered as they crept back up the hall. Maddie waved her to be quiet. Then she froze – more students were coming to the hall from the Gallery. Maddie grabbed Molly and the two of them scurried into a nearby janitor's closet. They stood there in the darkness as the last group of students passed and headed for the front of the building.

"It smells like onions in here," Molly whispered.

A voice answered, "I'm going to play football."

The girls yelped and burst out of the closet. Behind them a stocky boy with strong arms and curly hair stood next to the brooms and mops. "I'm going to play football," he repeated. Behind him stood Devon Walters.

Maddie put a hand to her chest. "Stout Burton, you almost gave me a heart attack! What are you two doing in there?"

"Hiding," Stout replied.

"Hiding," Devon repeated.

"Why?" Molly demanded.

"Because we have an assignment," Kate's voice answered.

Molly spun around. Kate came up the hall with Peter Dumfrey.

"Kate...Peter...Devon...what are you all doing here? What's going on?"

"There's no time to explain," Kate said. "We have to hurry before the Pug-Nasties get here."

"How do you know the Pug-Nasties are coming?"

"Oh, they're coming," Peter assured her. With Stout's help he stacked chairs against the wall. Then he stepped back and he shook his head. "That won't work," he sighed.

A clanking sound came from down the hall. Bair Burton appeared carrying a ladder.

"Ah, good," Peter said. "Just in time, Bair. These chairs aren't tall enough."

"Bair, what are you doing?" Molly inquired.

Bair just looked at her, his mouth hanging open.

"Over here, Bair," Devon directed. "We'll extend the ladder up the wall."

"Will someone please tell me what's going on?"

Kate pulled Molly aside. "Molly, things are moving faster than anyone expected. Mr. Holmes and Dr. Shelbourne figured out a way to get Ms. Bamcroft fired. That's the good news. But the bad news is that Dr. Shelbourne is now missing."

"What?!"

"Yes. And that's not all. Ms. Bamcroft stormed out of the building this morning madder than anyone has ever seen her. We don't know what she's going to do. She told all her teachers and all the Pug students to leave, so now the only ones left are the Laurentide students. But even most of them have gone home. With the building empty Mrs. Van Helsing is afraid the Pug-Nasties will try to steal the memorial cups again. So she sent us here to steal them first."

"Us?" Molly asked. "Who is us?"

"We're us," Peter replied. "We're the Guardian Team. Mrs. Van Helsing is a Guardian of Laurentide Academy and we're her helpers."

Molly stared dumbfounded at him.

"The cups," she said finally. "Why do they want the cups?"

"Because to travel they need silver," Peter informed her. "That's why the Pug-Nasties want the cups, so they can send a new group into the past to cause all kinds of mischief and destroy Laurentide Academy forever. We can't let them do that. Mrs. Van Helsing gave us our mission. Will you help, Molly?"

"You're all crazy," Molly replied.

"I'm bringing the ladder," Bair said suddenly. When Molly looked confused, Kate explained, "He's answering your question."

"That was, like, five minutes ago."

"He's slow."

Molly tried to wrap her thoughts around what was happening. "You all know Mrs. Van Helsing?" she asked.

"Yes, and we all have duties. I'm the Field Operator – that means I run errands. Maddie is Communications. Kate is Intelligence – that means she finds out what's going on. Devon is in charge of Transportation. Bair and Stout are Security."

"Security?"

"I'm going to play football," Stout answered. He dropped down into a crouch as though he were about to tackle someone.

"What does that have to do with security?" Molly asked him.

Stout smiled. "I'm good at tackling."

"Kate..."

"Not now, Molly," Kate urged. "We have to get these cups before..."

There was a crashing sound at the back of the building. Maddie rushed to the window.

"Here they come," she warned the others. "There are about twenty of them."

"Stout, go down and close the doors to the Gallery," Peter directed. "Bair, let's get that ladder higher on the wall."

Stout disappeared down the staircase. Bair and Devon put the ladder underneath the first oil painting at the end of the hall. It showed a student from the class of 1972 holding a silver cup. The girl looked out from the painting with a solemn gaze.

"Oh, my gosh!" Molly exclaimed. "That's Mrs. Van Helsing!"

"Yes," replied Kate. "You didn't know?"

"No. I only met her the other day."

"Mrs. Van Helsing received her cup back in 1972. All these students earned theirs, too."

Molly glanced down the row of portraits. After Mrs. Van Helsing's picture there was one of a student from 1950. After that was a student from 1944, then from the 1920s, and before that from 1909. The pictures went on and on until the first painting which showed a boy from 1869. All of them held silver cups, and except for Mrs. Van Helsing all the real cups from the pictures were mounted on small shelves next to their owner's portraits. There were ten in all.

"What are the cups for?" Molly asked as Devon climbed the ladder and retrieved the first one. He hurried back down to the floor where Bair then shifted the ladder to the next painting.

"Here," said Peter. He handed her the cup that Devon had retrieved. It was lightweight and smooth with a shine so clear Molly could see her reflection. She could also read the inscription: *"For Distinguished Service: 1893."* Above the words was an imprint of a train locomotive.

"That's two," Devon called. He tossed the second cup down to Peter, who caught it and put it in Molly's backpack. The boys slid the ladder down the wall for the next cup.

There was a tremendous smashing sound downstairs.

"Hurry, boys!" Maddie whispered.

Stout returned from the Gallery. "I locked the doors," he said. "But there are a lot of them. Bair, let's go beat 'em up!"

Bair grinned and turned to go but Devon grabbed him and put him back by the ladder.

"What's 1893?" Molly asked.

"That was the year of the Columbian Exposition," Kate explained. "All the cups were made from silver that Lady Shelbourne took to the Exposition, which was a world-wide celebration of freedom and progress held that year in Chicago."

"They all say the same thing?" Molly inquired, catching the third cup that Devon tossed down.

"Yes," said Peter. "All of them. And do you want to see something cool?" He took Molly's hand and led her down the hall to the oldest paintings. "Look," he pointed. "They've all got them."

Molly looked. "So?"

"So?" Peter repeated. "Use your head, dummy. I just said all the students in the paintings have the same silver cups with the same inscription: *For distinguished service: 1893.* They ALL have that."

Molly was about to say So? again when suddenly she understood. The student from the Class of 1885, the student from the Class of 1878, and the student from the class of 1869 all carried cups – from the Columbian Exposition of 1893.

"Huh?" she said. "They're holding cups that hadn't been made yet. How is that possible?"

Peter was about to reply when there was more crashing from the bottom of the stairs. Stout raced down to the Gallery.

"They knocked down the statues," he reported back. "And they're throwing pieces at the doors. That won't work. Boy, those Puggies are stupid."

Maddie looked outside. "They may be stupid," she said. "But they don't give up. Look!"

In the courtyard a Pug-Nasty led one of the stable horses to the back door of the Academy. The horse pulled a wagon full of hay. Other Pug-Nasties swarmed around the cart, grabbing hay and taking it inside the building. When the cart was empty another Pug-Nasty appeared carrying a match.

"That's the gypsy I chased!" Molly exclaimed.

The burglar looked up and recognized her, too. He opened his big mouth and screamed, a scream so loud that even inside the hall the students covered their ears. When the screaming stopped, they looked out again to see the burglar holding up his hand. The match was now lighted.

"Oh, no," Kate said. "They're going to burn down the doors!"

"Boys," Maddie called. "You really need to hurry."

Bair was very strong. He could move the ladder by himself but there were enormous bookcases below each painting that got in his way. It took time to put the ladder in just the right spot. When he did, Devon would scamper up to the highest rung, step out onto the top of the bookcase, and creep to the far end where each silver cup was mounted on a small shelf. He would collect the cup and then climb down. It was all taking too much time.

"We've got three," Peter announced. "Only seven more to go."

"We don't have time," Molly warned him. "You need to move faster."

"We can't. It's dangerous."

Just then a column of smoke floated up the staircase. From downstairs they heard wild cheering and some equally wild coughing.

"I'll call the fire department," Kate said, and ran up the hall toward the teachers' office.

"And the police," Molly called after her.

"Four," Devon announced, tossing a cup down to Stout. He jumped to the ladder and climbed down.

But just then came a stupendous crash from the Gallery. Great billows of smoke poured up the stairs. This time leaping, jumping figures came with it.

"Pug-Nasties!" Maddie screamed. She turned to run but the long-haired creatures in their tattered waistcoats were too fast for her. They rocketed up the stairs, leaped over the railing, and tackled her. One of them raised a big, powerful fist.

"Hike!" a voice bellowed, and out of the smoke a stocky figure exploded at a full run. The Pug-Nasty looked up just in time to see Stout hurtling toward him like a cannon ball. Stout crashed into the creature and sent him sailing across the hall.

"22, 47, 18...hut...hut...hike!" Stout yelled, and charged into another gypsy, hitting him so hard that the creature did a complete somersault before falling flat on his face.

"Football, I love it!!" Stout shouted, and ran about the hall knocking over Pug-Nasties one after another. The ones who had made it into the hall began to retreat. But others came up the stairs and soon there were too many of them for Stout to handle.

"Maddie, run," Peter said, helping her to her feet. "Get Kate and the two of you wait by the front door. The rest of us will catch up when we have all the cups."

Maddie hurried away just as two Pug-Nasties came up the stairs and leaped right over Stout. They charged down the hall and made straight for Molly who was at the bottom of the ladder. They were so focused on her they didn't notice Peter, who grabbed a mop from the closet and swung it like a baseball bat, knocking the two burglars head over heels.

"Thank you, Peter!" Molly called.

"You're welcome," he answered. "Too bad I didn't have a pooper-scooper!"

More Pug-Nasties came up the stairs. Molly threw open the doors to a bookcase and started pulling out volumes of an encyclopedia. She loved books and normally wouldn't use one as a weapon but this was an emergency.

"Take that!" she cried, and threw one of the biggest books at a gypsy who jumped over Peter and tried to chase Devon up the ladder. The book hit the creature on the side of the head and knocked him cold. "And here's one for you!" she yelled, throwing another volume at the next gypsy. One after another she knocked the Pug-Nasties down, defending the hallway using books as her missiles. The Pug-Nasties were loud and strong, she learned, but they weren't brave. The more she struck with a book, the more the rest hid behind pillars to avoid being hit. Peter dashed back to help her, and then Stout, and together they held off two dozen of the creatures while Devon and Bair moved the ladder.

"We can't hold them!" Peter cried. "We're running out of encyclopedias. We need to get the rest of the cups."

Suddenly the biggest Pug-Nasty leaped up the stairs with a horrible scream. He surprised everyone, including Devon who slipped from the ladder and fell.

"Ow!" he cried out. "Peter, I hurt my ankle!"

Peter backed up to help but as soon as he did the crowd of Pug-Nasties surged forward. "I can't," he called. "We're going to have to leave the cups."

"Oh, no we don't," Stout replied. He dropped down into a crouch. "Football!" he yelled and charged into the Pug-Nasties.

He knocked over several but there were too many of them. They quickly overwhelmed him and Stout disappeared under an enormous pile of screaming, punching gypsies. Peter went to help him but he, too, was knocked down. A Pug-Nasty even started to drag him away.

"Help!" he called.

Suddenly the Pug-Nasty let go of Peter's foot. He had to because Bair grabbed him by his long hair and picked him up right off the ground.

"Aaiiieiee!" the Pug-Nasty screamed as Bair swung him around and around and then threw him through a door into one of the classrooms.

"Get off of my brother," Bair growled at the pile of Pug-Nasties who were trying to hold Stout down. One by one he picked them up and threw them across the hall.

Molly was wondering how she could help when suddenly she saw the biggest gypsy of them all, the one she had chased across the lawn, pull himself away from the crowd. He leaped to the top of a locker and then from there to the nearest bookcase. He waved at the smoke, trying to see where he was. Then he saw Molly standing by herself.

Molly looked at the burglar, then at the ladder, then at the six remaining silver cups that were still on their shelves high above each bookcase. There was a gap between each bookcase – a gap with a fifteen-foot drop. Without taking time to think, she leaped for the ladder.

"Peter!" she called.

"Molly, what are you doing?"

"Playing catch," she yelled down. "And I need help!"

She climbed as fast as she could to the top of the first bookcase and jumped off the ladder. The big Pug-Nasty saw her. He screamed and jumped from his bookcase to the next one in line. From there he ran after her, jumping from one bookcase to the next.

"Oh, now I've done it," Molly whispered. She turned and ran, too, as fast as she could right to the end of her own bookcase. "Up, up, up!" she cried and jumped.

She made it! She landed on top of the next bookcase, grabbed the silver cup there, and tossed it down to Peter.

"Next!" she yelled, and ran and jumped again. Five more times she ran across the top of the bookcases, jumping from one to another and sweeping the silver cups off their shelves as she did. Peter ran alongside down on the floor, catching each cup as it fell and stuffing it into her backpack. The big Pug-Nasty was right behind her all the way, screaming in anger as each time he got to the silver cups too late.

"Got'em!" Peter yelled when he had all the cups. "You're at the end of the hall, Molly. Jump!"

Molly ran across the last bookcase and threw herself into the air. She barely caught one of the velvet drapes by the front staircase. It swung wildly and almost tore away from the ceiling but she held on tight and slid down to the floor.

The gypsy jumped for the same curtain but missed. He hit the wall and fell with a thud right next to Bair, who came running up.

"I don't like you," Bair said to him. He picked up the big Pug-Nasty and stuffed him into a locker, then slammed the door.

Maddie came up the staircase.

"Guys, come on! The smoke is getting worse," she said, but then she looked in horror behind Bair and Stout. The back half of Students Hall was all on fire. It was so bad the Pug-Nasties were jumping out of windows to get away.

"Run!" Peter cried.

Together the students rushed down the stairs, with Peter helping Devon who hobbled on a twisted ankle. Kate hurried them across the lobby and outside onto the lawn.

"Is everyone here?" Peter asked. "Devon, Kate, Maddie, Molly, Bair, Stout...good, we're all safe."

The whole school was in flames. Fire and smoke poured out of every opening. In the distance they heard sirens.

"The firemen will be too late," Kate said tearfully.

"But what about the Pug-Nasties?" Maddie asked. "Are they trapped inside?"

In answer to her question they heard screams and laughter. From behind the Academy the hay wagon appeared, racing at top speed as the horse galloped to get away from the burning school. In the wagon were the Pug-Nasties, whooping and hollering and waving flaming torches.

"Get out of the way!"

The students leaped aside to keep from being run over. Molly barely missed being trampled under the hooves of the panicked horse. But as she dove to safety, a hand reached down and snatched her backpack.

"My bag!" Molly cried. "The cups!"

She chased after the wagon but the horse was too fast. The Pug-Nasties raced across the lawn and reached the open gate just before the fire trucks rushed in. They turned left up the road toward Pug.

"We've lost them!"

"Yes, but look."

The Pug-Nasties went up the Pug Road but then turned as they passed The Hedges. With loud cries they made the horse gallop off the road and into the empty fields behind the tall bushes.

One by one the creatures threw their torches. And one by one The Hedges caught fire.

"Oh, no!" cried Kate. "They're starting another fire. They're going to burn down the whole town!"

Even as the fire trucks hurried up to the burning school, the students watched a second disaster start. The Hedges were bone dry. So were the fields. Worse, there was an ill wind coming over the hill from Pug that fed the flames and pushed them straight toward town.

"What are we going to do?" Maddie asked.

Firemen jumped from the trucks and sprayed water on the Academy but the heat was so great they could barely get close. Part of the roof caved in, sending up a shower of sparks.

"Molly," Maddie said again. "What are we going to do?"

Molly didn't know. Her school was burning down and now on the other side of the road an equally large fire was just getting started. She tried to think – and then she remembered what Maddie herself had told her to do in moments like this.

"I know what we're going to do," she announced to her panicked friends. "Stop thinking. Start moving. We have to get out of here and warn the town. Everybody, RUN!"

CHAPTER 9

A Ticket to Ride

THE STUDENTS HAD no trouble warning people. Everyone in Laurentide was outdoors, watching smoke billow into the sky from the fire at the Academy. Soon they noticed more smoke on the north side of town.

"There's a fire in The Hedges!" Molly called out as she ran toward home.

"There's a fire in The Hedges!" Peter yelled as he raced to his father's store.

Soon the flames in The Hedges were ten stories tall. People began packing up their things.

"Molly! Thank goodness you're here," Aunt Marcy exclaimed as Molly burst through the front door. "There's a fire at the Academy."

"No, Aunt Marcy," Molly replied, fighting back tears. "There is no more Academy. It's all on fire. And the Pug-Nasties set fire to The Hedges, too."

"The what?"

"The Pug-Nasties. The gypsies, the burglars – whatever they are. They work for Ursula Bamcroft and they're destroying the school and the whole town and whoever won't let them be in charge."

Aunt Marcy took Molly in her arms. "There, there," she said. "You're just upset. It can't be that bad. I'm sure the Academy will be fine. And we're safe here at home."

But just then a fire engine roared to the end of the street. The field there was a raging inferno.

"There's a fire there, too!" Aunt Marcy said in surprise.

"I told you," said Molly.

"Oh, my. Oh, my."

A police car followed the fire engine. The officer spoke over his loudspeaker.

"*Everyone on Linden Street. Evacuate your houses. Evacuate the neighborhood.*"

"What does evacuate mean?" Molly asked.

"It means we must leave," Aunt Marcy explained. "Go upstairs and pack. I'll get your brother ready. We can go to the Town Square until the firemen put the fire out."

Molly hurried upstairs to her room and pulled a suitcase out of the closet. But then she didn't know what to put in it. "How long are we going downtown?" she called. "Do I need my pajamas?"

"Molly, just hurry!" Aunt Marcy replied. "Grab the most valuable things and let's go. The fire is getting closer."

Molly ran to the window. The fire *was* getting closer. It had spread from the fields to the beautiful linden trees at the end of the street. The firefighters were helping people to escape.

She spun around and looked at her room, realizing that her house might actually burn down. What should she save? Her toys, her dolls, her trophies from soccer, her t-shirt collection? She didn't want to lose anything.

Two minutes later she was back downstairs, dragging the suitcase. Aunt Marcy had Michael in her arms.

"Molly! Why is your suitcase so heavy? What have you got in there?"

"All my books," Molly replied.

"Your books! You need clothes and your toothbrush, not something to read."

"Grandpa says books are the most valuable things," Molly explained.

"Oh, there's no time to argue. Come get in the car."

But the street was so packed with people Aunt Marcy couldn't get their car out of the driveway. People blew their horns and yelled at each other.

"Everyone!" the policeman called out. He stood on the roof of his car. "Everyone listen to me. Get out of your cars and leave the area. You must go *now*."

"We'll have to walk," Aunt Marcy said. "Oh, your father isn't going to like it if anything happens to his car..."

They jumped out and hurried down the sidewalk, with Aunt Marcy carrying Michael.

"Are we coming back? Are the firemen going to stop the fire in time?"

Aunt Marcy glanced over her shoulder.

"I'm afraid time is running out for us, sweetie."

They reached the end of the block. It seemed like every family in town was on the street, pushing strollers and carts and suitcases down the road. From the middle of the avenue Molly could look west toward Laurentide Academy. There was a raging fire in the distance that she knew used to be her school. Tears ran down her cheeks. Thanks a lot, Ms. Bamcroft, she thought. Now everyone is going to be equal, alright. Equally miserable.

Town Square was filled with people. Children cried and adults looked worried. Dogs ran around barking at the smoke.

Peter arrived carrying three empty leashes. He looked exhausted.

"Molly, thank goodness I found you."

"Peter, are you okay?"

"I'm okay. But I've been busy. We're moving all the animals. My dad has a truck and we're going to get them all on the ferry. I just took some dogs down to the dock."

"You're going across the river?"

"*Everyone* is going across the river. Look."

People were starting to leave the square and head to the docks.

"We're leaving town?" Molly asked Aunt Marcy.

"It looks like we'll have to, sweetie. Come on, let's follow the crowd."

"Um, Aunt Marcy," Peter piped up. "My dad and I need help with the animals. Can Molly come with me to get them loaded onto the truck?"

"Oh, no, Peter. Things are much too crazy right now. I must keep Molly with me."

"But we really need help," Peter pleaded. "The animals are scared. Molly could be a great help – and we'll be on the same ferry as you, in the big pet store truck."

"I thought you said the animals were already loaded," Molly whispered.

"Shh!"

Aunt Marcy thought for a moment. She loved animals.

"Okay, Peter. Molly can go with you. But Molly, make absolutely sure you stay with Mr. Dumfrey and get on the ferry with him. I'll see you there in half an hour, okay? Don't make me have a heart attack by having to look for you."

"Okay," said Molly.

"I'll see you soon," Aunt Marcy said. She headed for the river. Michael waved to Molly over her shoulder.

"Peter, what are you doing?"

"We have to go get Mrs. Van Helsing," Peter told her as they hurried across the square.

"Isn't she in her store?"

"No, she and Mr. Van Helsing are at home. So we're going to get her."

"But they live up on Washington Street! The fire must be there by now."

"Only barely," Peter said. "Mr. Van Helsing called and said cars can still get through."

"But we don't have a car," Molly reminded him. "And we have to help your dad with the animals."

"Dad already has the animals loaded," Peter told her. "And you're right – we don't have a car. But we have this!"

They arrived at the pet shop. In front of it was a gleaming new fire engine!

"Where did you get a fire engine?!" Molly gasped.

"The mayor was hiding it at his house," Peter explained. "The firemen found it and brought it down here to help with the fire. But they've all left to help at the ferry. Now we need it to help the Van Helsings."

"But if the firemen are gone, who's going to drive it?"

Devon stuck his head out of the window of the fire engine cab.

"All aboard!" he yelled. "Get a move on, guys."

"Devon can drive a fire engine?" Molly asked. She jumped up into the back seat and found Bair, Kate, and Maddie already there. Stout was in front with Devon.

"I guess we'll find out," Peter said. "Wait, Devon." He ran into the pet store and came out with his school backpack. "Okay, let's go!"

Devon started the engine with a roar. Stout turned on the flashing lights and the siren. Molly held on as the truck started to move.

"I've never ridden in a fire engine before," she said to Bair.

"That's okay," Devon told her. "I've never driven one before."

They drove up Early Street and away from the square. It was eerie how empty the neighborhoods were now that everyone had fled to the river.

"Hurry up, Devon!" Peter shouted. He climbed to the top of the truck and looked out. "The fire is getting worse."

"I'm hurrying," Devon replied. He wrenched the big steering wheel as they turned onto Coolidge Way. The truck bounced over a curb, tossing everyone in their seats.

"Oops," Devon said. "Sorry."

He turned the wheel back but now he knocked over a light pole.

"Stay on the road, Devon!"

"I'm trying!"

Finally he got the fire engine going straight. For two blocks they had no trouble. Bair finally said to Molly, "Me, neither." Then Devon looked up ahead. Somebody had abandoned two cars in the middle of the road.

"Uh-oh. Peter, the road is blocked," Devon called. "We'll have to go another way."

"No," said Peter. "We don't have time."

"But how are we going to get past the cars?"

Next to him Stout sounded two mighty blasts on the air horn. "Football!" he yelled.

"If you say so," Devon shrugged. He stepped on the accelerator and roared down the street directly at the abandoned cars. The fire engine hit them at full speed. The cars flew this way and that and the truck barreled right through. Stout laughed out loud.

Devon moaned, "I'll never get a driver's license now."

They reached Washington Street and the Van Helsing house. Mr. and Mrs. Van Helsing waited outside, holding handkerchiefs over their mouths because of the smoke. Mr. Van Helsing carried a suitcase, his wife carried her leather satchel. All around them the neighborhood was on fire. The noise of the flames was a roar like an approaching train.

"Thank goodness you're here," Mr. Van Helsing said. "Peter, take these bags. Bair, help me with Mrs. Van Helsing."

They lifted Mrs. Van Helsing up to the cab. She squeezed in next to Molly.

"Oh, this is horrible," she said, coughing. "The noise, the smoke – who would think I would live to see something like this twice?"

Molly was going to ask her what she meant but Mr. Van Helsing climbed up and squeezed between them. "Good job, Devon," he said. "I'll drive now." He slid behind the wheel and backed the fire engine down the street.

"Dearest, what time is it?" Mrs. Van Helsing asked her husband.

"It's 7:30pm, my love. We can still make it – if that's what you want to do."

"That's what we *must* do," his wife declared. But then she was seized with a fit of coughing. When it stopped she was barely able to look out the window.

"It won't work," she whispered. "I don't have the strength."

"What won't work?" Molly asked.

Mrs. Van Helsing looked at her. "Molly, I must ask you a big favor."

"Okay."

"I have to ask you to do something that will be difficult and maybe dangerous. But you can do it. I believe you can. If you succeed you can stop this fire. You can make it as though it never happened."

"I can save my house?" Molly asked. "I can save my school? How?"

Mrs. Van Helsing reached into the satchel and pulled out the train ticket. She thrust it into Molly's hand and closed her fingers around it.

"Take this," Mrs. Van Helsing said. "It will get you on the train. You can stop Ursula Bamcroft and you can stop this fire."

Molly wondered what to say. She felt so sorry for this poor, sick woman who still thought there was a train somewhere to catch.

"Mrs. Van Helsing, there isn't..."

"Don't worry. There will be someone to help you. She'll know what to do."

"But I..."

"Please," Mrs. Van Helsing pleaded. "Promise me you'll go."

Molly bit her lip. This was all so crazy. "I promise," she said.

Mr. Van Helsing slammed on the brakes and the truck skidded to a halt. A huge linden tree lay across the road.

"Whoaaa!" said Peter. "That's a big tree."

"It sure is," said Mr. Van Helsing. "And it's blocking the last open road to the train station."

He backed up but couldn't find another way to go. "We can't get through, my love," he announced. "The streets to the station are blocked..."

"And there's why!" Maddie cried. "Look!"

Down the street they saw Pug-Nasties running and jumping along, staying one step ahead of the fire. They carried axes and chopped down every tree they could find to block the road.

Peter stuck his head in the window. "See!" he said to Molly. "They're trying to stop us from getting to the station. They know about the train."

"Dearest, we must get through," Mrs. Van Helsing told her husband. "Molly will go in my place but she must get to that train."

"Well, she can't get there on this fire truck," Mr. Van Helsing apologized.

"Maybe not," Devon said. "But I'm still in charge of transportation and I'm not giving up."

He hopped down to the street and limped behind a house that had flames leaping from its roof. Disappearing into the back yard, he reappeared on a bicycle.

"Bair, Stout, Peter, there are more bikes back there," Devon called. The boys followed his order and quickly returned with bicycles. "Molly, ride with Peter. You have a train to catch."

"Boys, get to the station and then meet us in Town Square," Mr. Van Helsing told them, revving the engine on the truck. "From there we'll go to the ferry together."

Molly climbed onto the back of Peter's bike. "Your backpack is in the way," she told him.

"Then you carry it," he replied. "Hang on."

"Good luck, Molly!" Kate yelled as the fire engine drove away. Molly didn't even have time to wave to her friend. She hung on for dear life as Peter steered his bike around the burning tree and pedaled as fast as he could down the street. Devon, Bair, and Stout followed close behind.

The Pug-Nasties waved their axes and screamed.

"Uh-oh, they see us," Devon called. "Go left. I know a shortcut."

The boys turned into an alley, pedaling like mad. Molly looked over her shoulder and saw the Pug-Nasties chasing after them, running and jumping like kangaroos down the narrow alley.

"Right!" Devon yelled. "Turn right!"

They raced between two burning houses, across a garden, and out onto Early Street. Behind them one of the Pug-Nasties ran into a clothesline. Another tripped over a garden gnome. But the others were getting closer.

"Peter, go ahead," Devon ordered. "Stout, come with me."

Devon and Stout turned their bikes around and charged back at their pursuers.

"Football!" Stout shouted as he crashed his bike into the Pug-Nasties. The axes went flying and a huge fight began.

Peter, Molly, and Bair continued down one more street. Smoke was everywhere. Finally they caught a glimpse of the clock tower on the train station.

"Almost there!" Peter said.

No sooner were the words out of his mouth than they had to stop. The street was covered with branches and garbage cans that the Pug-Nasties had spread everywhere.

"We can still make it," Peter panted, jumping off the bike. "The station is just over..."

He was interrupted by a loud creaking and groaning. The old oak tree at the end of Early Street was on fire from the ground up to its tallest branch and its trunk was about to give way. It was a massive tree, the largest in town. If it fell it would block the street from even a chipmunk getting through.

Bair ran forward. A stop sign lay in the road and he picked it up. Using it as a lever, he pushed against the tree. Peter hurried to help him.

"Molly, go!" Peter told her.

Molly went forward but stopped. She could barely see around the corner.

"By myself?" she asked. "Aren't you coming with me?"

"No," Peter grunted, pushing against Bair who pushed against the tree. "There's only one ticket."

"But the fire... How do I...? What will happen to you?"

"We'll run to the ferry. Just go – we can't hold this forever..."

The oak began to lean. Molly didn't have time to delay. She ran forward and passed under the tree.

"Peter!" she remembered. "I still have your backpack!"

Through the smoke she heard him yell, "Keep it! You'll need it."

With that the mighty oak crashed to the ground, shaking the neighborhood. Sparks flew everywhere. Molly screamed. Embers landed in her hair and she brushed at them frantically.

"Peter!" she called. "Bair!"

But there was no answer from the other side of the fire. Molly prayed the boys had gotten away in time. Tightening the straps on the backpack, she turned and ran as fast as she could down the old railroad tracks.

"Oh, let there be someone at the station," she thought. "Let there be someone there..."

Then through the smoke she saw the station – and there was in fact someone there.

A man in a blue conductor's uniform stood on the platform. He studied a pocket watch while listening calmly to a prim young lady next to him. She wore a long skirt, a herringbone riding jacket, and a deerstalker cap and seemed to take no notice at all of the fire which had almost reached the station. But the lady's composure was not what surprised Molly. No, what surprised Molly completely and made her stop still was the train.

"There's a train!" she exclaimed, and her mouth dropped open in shock.

There was indeed a train. A vintage steam locomotive leading five cars sat idling outside Mrs. Walters' coffee shop. They pointed down a long line of tracks that Molly had never noticed before, tracks that were gleaming and new and that stretched as far as she could see through the business district and down to the far side of town and then on out to the horizon.

"There's a train!" she said again. "And tracks! When did they build those?"

Just then the house behind her burst into flames. With a crackle and a roar fire climbed to the roof and jumped to the building next door. It was heading toward the station.

Molly shrieked and took off running again. The conductor and the lady turned and saw her for the first time as Molly charged down the tracks, leaped to the platform, and came skidding to a halt before them.

"Please take me with you," she gasped. "I have a ticket."

The young lady turned out to be a girl only a few years older than Molly. She was as surprised to see Molly as Molly was to see the train. She looked at the conductor, who looked at Molly, who looked at both of them.

"There's a train," Molly added, not knowing what else to say.

"Good evening," the girl in the herringbone jacket said with a soft English accent. "Yes, there is a train. It's a train station."

"And I have a ticket," Molly repeated.

"You do indeed have a ticket. Ah...may I ask, where did you get this?" The young lady took the ticket gently from Molly's hand, studied it, and handed it to the conductor who did the same.

"Mrs. Van Helsing gave it to me," Molly panted.

"And where is Isabelle Van Helsing?"

"Well, right now she should be getting on a boat," Molly said anxiously. She looked toward the river but couldn't see past the town square because of the smoke. "She's sick. She has really bad asthma and said to tell you that she couldn't come tonight and she gave me her ticket and Peter Dumfrey and Bair and Kate and all of us went to her house in the fire truck to pick her up and take her to the boat so I hope they all got there in time."

"Who is Peter Dumfrey?" the conductor asked.

"His dad owns the pet shop," Molly explained.

"Pet shop?" the girl asked. "Fire truck? This is highly unusual."

Molly looked around her. Her entire world was burning down and now a train had appeared out of nowhere. "Yeah," she admitted. "My whole week is turning out to be highly unusual, actually. Can we go?"

The conductor shook his head. "It is only six minutes to eight," he said, holding out his watch. "The *Jeremy Bentham* is the eight o'clock train and it does not leave until eight o'clock. We must be timely."

"But the fire is getting closer!" Molly insisted. She pointed to the houses along the railroad tracks. As they watched, the one closest to the station collapsed in a ball of fire. Weeds along the tracks began to smolder.

The conductor refused to budge.

"We must not leave early," he said flatly.

"Not even in an emergency?" Molly asked.

"Not even in an emergency. If one is careless with time things can happen quite unpredictably. Someone must keep order and that is what I do. I am the conductor."

"In a minute you'll be a candle if we don't get out of here," Molly pointed out.

Hot ashes landed in the gutters and set the nests alight. The pigeons flew away, scattering burning twigs onto the platform. Molly hurried around to stamp them out.

"Perhaps, Mr. Stewart," the girl in the riding coat suggested carefully, her eyes on the burning weeds, "perhaps just this once we could make an exception..."

"Out of the question," the conductor declared. But even as he spoke he walked down the platform to the last passenger car, the one that had been at the station for years but that was now painted a glossy forest green and had the name *Pullman #74* written in bold yellow paint above the windows. A piece of burning straw had lodged in the window trim. Mr. Stewart wet his fingers, plucked out the straw, and dropped it to the ground where it burned itself out. Then he wiped away the scorch mark left on the car.

"But you must admit, this is a highly unusual situation," the girl commented. She stepped to the end of the platform and looked up the tracks as though hoping to see the fires burn themselves out, or perhaps hoping that Mrs. Van Helsing would appear after all.

"And it will be more unusual if we do not leave on time," the conductor reminded her. "Five more minutes."

Molly grew frantic. Fire crawled across the roof of the station. The smoke was so thick she coughed. The young lady handed her a lace handkerchief and Molly held it over her mouth.

"Thanth yuuth," she said through the handkerchief.

"You're welcome," the girl replied. "Mr. Stewart, I..." she began to say, but at that moment the clock tower fell over with a crash. The girl grabbed Molly and pulled her to safety as it slid across the roof and smashed down onto the platform. Flaming boards flew everywhere. Some slid under the parlor car where despite his best efforts Mr. Stewart could not reach them. Smoke rose from beneath the train.

"Mr. Stewart!" the girl in the coat said sharply. "Now I must insist. The *Jeremy Bentham* itself is in danger. We need to leave immediately!"

Mr. Stewart brushed ashes from his jacket and wiped his brow with a handkerchief of his own. There was no denying the situation was serious.

"By the good queen's crown," he sputtered. "This is most unusual. I've never heard of anything like it but...well, you are right. If we do not go now we may never leave at all. Very well. Hurry now, on the train with you. On the train!"

Molly followed the girl aboard the parlor car. She looked back just in time to see the windows of Mrs. Walters' coffee shop burst outward from the heat. Poor Mrs. Walters, she thought. She had worked so hard to have a business of her own.

Mr. Stewart blew a long blast of his whistle. Up front the locomotive responded with a great burst of steam and a loud whistle of its own.

Down at the river the ferry started to move away from the dock.

"Wait!" a voice shouted.

Peter and Bair ran down the pier and leaped aboard. As Devon helped them to their feet, they heard the steam whistle echo across town.

"What in the world is that?" someone asked.

"It's a train whistle," Mrs. Van Helsing replied.

"But there's no train in Laurentide."

Mrs. Van Helsing smiled. "There is now."

At the station a *chug-chug-chug* arose from the locomotive as the wheels began to turn.

"All aboard!!" Mr. Stewart called. With careful steps he walked along the platform, checking each door of the train. At the last car he swung himself aboard.

Up front, the locomotive with **Jeremy Bentham** stenciled across its nose spouted an enormous cloud of steam and pulled its way across Union Street. The cars behind lurched and clacked and followed smartly, the gleaming carriage wheels rolling smoothly across the polished rails. The last coach cleared the station just as the front wall of the waiting room – ticket window and all – collapsed and fell onto the tracks. By mere seconds, Molly and her companions had gotten away safely. The *Jeremy Bentham* was on its way.

Mr. Stewart checked his watch a final time.

It was one minute before eight o'clock.

CHAPTER 10

Veronica T. Boone

THE YOUNG LADY turned from the window.

"I am Veronica T. Boone," she introduced herself. "And we are going to make things right."

Molly could not even respond. She trembled from her narrow escape. Even more, she was on a train for the first time in her life – and this train looked like nothing she had ever imagined.

The coach they were in had slender chairs atop an oriental rug. There was a card table made of marble and a sofa with needlework pillows. The walls were mahogany, the curtains were lace. Two chandeliers hung from the ceiling. In the corner was a piano – a piano! – and next to it an exquisite bookcase with glass doors. Finally, a small dining table sat in the middle of the room, set with silver and china and little cucumber sandwiches arranged for a snack.

"Mr. Stewart," Veronica said. "Once we are up to speed, perhaps Higgins could bring some fresh tea. I'm sure we're all thirsty."

"I don't drink tea," Molly managed to say.

"Some lemonade, then?"

"Yes, thank you."

"Very good, Miss Veronica," Mr. Stewart said. "And I shall check with the Navigator to confirm our arrival."

Mr. Stewart left through a door at the front of the coach. Molly recovered her senses.

"I'm on a train," she said in amazement.

"You are indeed," Veronica T. Boone smiled. "And not just any train. You are on the *Jeremy Bentham*, the most reliable, most comfortable, and most timely train in all the Shelbourne holdings."

"Shelbourne?" Molly gasped. "Are you Lady Shelbourne?"

Veronica giggled. "No, silly. I told you, I am Veronica T. Boone. But Lady Shelbourne has allowed us to use the *Jeremy Bentham* when needed. In fact, she insisted on it. So you are quite welcome here."

"But I've never met Lady Shelbourne," Molly said.

"And she has never met you," Veronica agreed. "But she knew you would come along one day, or someone very much like you. Lady Shelbourne counts on good people to keep the bad people from making a perfect mess of the world."

"I don't understand," Molly said.

"You will. Shall we eat something first? Then we can talk. And we can start with you telling me your name."

"I'm Molly."

Veronica smiled. "I am very pleased to meet you, Molly."

They sat at the table and ate sandwiches while the countryside rolled by. For a while it was farmland that Molly recognized but as the train went faster and faster the land disappeared entirely and the train rolled onto a high bridge where fog rolled in thick clouds beneath them.

"I can't see the ground," Molly commented. "Are we in the mountains?"

"No," Veronica replied, nibbling her sandwich. "We're over the Chasm."

"The what?"

"It's the gap between now and then," Veronica explained. "It's terribly deep and rather long. We'll be crossing it for a while."

"Crossing it to where? And what's at the bottom?"

"I'm not sure there is a bottom. Even if there is, you don't want to go there."

"Why not?"

"Because if you do you'll be lost to history."

Mr. Stewart returned with a man who carried a silver tray.

"Fresh lemonade, Miss Veronica."

"Oh, thank you, Higgins. Molly, may I introduce you to Higgins? He is simply the very best chef on any train anywhere."

"I am pleased to meet you, Miss Molly," Higgins said with a bow. He wore a chef's coat and a black bow tie.

"I'm pleased to meet you, too, Mr. Higgins," Molly said. "Thank you for the sandwiches. They're delicious."

"Do you really think so?" Higgins asked.

"Oh, yes," Molly told him. "Something happened to the crusts, though. There aren't any."

"Of course not. We cut them off," Higgins explained.

"Why?"

Higgins thought about that. "I don't know. That's just what we do."

"I'm not much of a cook but I bake a little," Molly told him. "My mom says I make the best pancakes in town."

"Pancakes?" Higgins said. "What are pancakes?"

"Oh my gosh, you don't know what pancakes are?"

"Is it a cake in a pan?"

"No, it's not in a pan," Molly explained. "You pour the batter onto a griddle."

"You do what?"

"You pour the batter...look, it'll be easier if I show you. Where's your kitchen?"

"Molly," Veronica interrupted. "Focus, please. We have more important things than pancakes right now. And don't go giving Higgins any ideas. The next thing you know he'll be changing a menu that has served perfectly well for over a hundred years."

"Now, Miss Veronica, a little variety is good now and then."

"Not with breakfast, Higgins."

"Yes, well, if you'll excuse me, I must return to the galley and plan for the morning." Higgins bowed. "It is a pleasure to meet you, Miss Molly."

"It's nice to meet you, too, Mr. Higgins. Don't forget – let's make pancakes sometime."

Mr. Stewart cleared his throat.

"Ahem. Miss Veronica, I've spoken with the Navigator and as I feared there will be a problem reaching our destination."

Veronica looked up. "What manner of problem, Mr. Stewart? I asked for a straight journey to Chicago."

"We're going to Chicago?" Molly exclaimed. "Awesome! My mother is there. I could visit my grandparents – although my clothes are a mess." She sniffed her sleeve and used the butter knife to study her reflection. "My clothes smell like smoke and I've got soot all over my face. My grandparents will think I've gone mad."

"One can understand their confusion," Mr. Stewart muttered. "But back to the schedule...as I mentioned at the station, one must be careful with time or it will behave unpredictably. And despite my best efforts we did not leave the station in a timely manner. We departed early."

"Are you saying we will not be able to get to Chicago?" Veronica asked.

"Oh, we will arrive in Chicago," Mr. Stewart assured her. "But not when we intended."

"We're going to arrive late?" Molly asked.

"No," Mr. Stewart said. "We will arrive early. We will pull into the station in 1952."

Molly's mouth dropped open. Veronica was annoyed.

"Mr. Stewart," she said sharply. "I remember distinctly telling you we had a simple schedule to keep."

"Yes, Miss Veronica. But I told *you* we needed to be timely."

"I understand. But we did not know about the Laurentide fire and it was imperative to leave before any damage was done to the *Jeremy Bentham*."

"I agree, miss. But when you act in haste there are consequences. We acted in haste and our consequence now is that we are on an untimely journey."

"And what does that mean, exactly?"

Mr. Stewart bowed his head. "I am embarrassed to say I do not know. I have never been on an untimely journey. None of us have. The Navigator is quite agitated and would only tell me that if we want to go to Chicago tomorrow we can only arrive there in 1952. Parts of the journey are out of his control. Now, if you'll excuse me, I must inspect the other cars."

Mr. Stewart left. Veronica sipped her tea, thinking.

"Is Mr. Stewart crazy?" Molly asked.

"Of course not. Why would you say such a thing?"

"He's talking about traveling through time."

"Yes."

"But that's impossible."

"I certainly hope not," said Veronica. "Our journey is shaping up to be difficult enough as it is."

"But why does he think we're going to be in Chicago tomorrow in 1952? That's crazy."

Veronica set down her cup. "Molly, sometimes it is helpful to be direct. But if you are too direct it is rude. Let's not be too direct, shall we? Mr. Stewart is not crazy. He is the conductor and a Timekeeper. He is here to ensure that nothing bad happens to the *Jeremy Bentham* and to do his best to see it stays on time. We must do *our* best to help him."

"But what about traveling through time?"

"What about it? It's simply a matter of speed."

"Huh?"

"Molly, you know of course that Lady Shelbourne received her inheritance from her father, who was a very rich man. Do you remember how Lord Shelbourne became wealthy?"

"Mrs. Van Helsing said he owned a coal mine. And railroads."

"Yes, he made his fortune in England in the coal industry. Later he built railroads. He used the coal from his mines to fuel the locomotives on his trains. Well, one day his miners accidentally dug into a small seam of silver running through one of his coal mines. No one noticed at first and the silver was accidentally mixed into the coal and thrown into the firebox on one of the company's locomotives. And do you know what happened? The train shot forward in time twenty years!"

"What!"

"Yes. Fortunately the engineer had the good sense to turn right around when he realized what happened. We can only imagine how history might have been disturbed if he and the passengers had stayed where they arrived."

"But how did it happen?" Molly asked.

"What the miners discovered," Veronica explained, "was something called anodized silver. It's a special kind of silver – lighter, shinier, and stronger than the regular metal. When mixed with coal it allows a train to travel not just fast, but fast enough to break the bonds of time. No one had ever found any before Lord Shelbourne and no one has found any since. During his lifetime Lord Shelbourne had the only supply of anodized silver and he kept it a secret. He realized he had something very special. He also saw that it was a power that needed to be guarded carefully."

"So," Molly said slowly, thinking things through. "The *Jeremy Bentham* travels through time using special coal in its engine?"

"Exactly so," said Veronica.

"But if all a train needs is the silver, why aren't they all traveling through time? You must be able to buy silver somewhere. Everyone could be traveling from one year to another. Think of the trips you could take!"

"Molly, you're not listening. It's not just any silver. It's *anodized* silver. Lord Shelbourne's miners found all they could find. After that there wasn't any more. They gave it to Lord Shelbourne who in turn left it as an inheritance to Lady Elizabeth."

"What did Lady Elizabeth do with it?"

"She kept it a secret, too. She decided that traveling through time was dangerous. If the wrong people did it, history would become very confused and people's lives could be in danger."

"So she hid the silver?"

"In a way, yes."

"What do you mean, in a way?" Molly asked.

Veronica sighed. "Lady Elizabeth knew she must keep the power of the silver a secret but she was still proud of her father for having discovered it. So she kept some of it to be used in the *Jeremy Bentham*. The rest she had made into silver cups."

"The silver Memorial Cups at Laurentide!" Molly guessed.

"Exactly so."

"But why? Why did she make the cups?"

"They were a gift."

"A gift? For who?"

"For whom," Veronica corrected her. "The cups were a gift for the world," she explained. "You must remember, this was over a hundred years ago. It was the 1800s – the *late* 1800s. It was a time of great progress. New things were being invented and built every day. Railroads, electricity, skyscrapers and bridges and grand ocean liners. People were hopeful and optimistic that they could do anything. After all, the world had come a long way from the days when everyone was poor and never traveled and lived a short, hard life. America, especially, had come a long way. Why, it was only four hundred years before that Christopher Columbus had discovered America. Back in 1492 America was a wild land of forests and fields. But by 1892 it was the richest country in the world and getting better every day. The world wanted to celebrate. America wanted to celebrate. It wanted to show the world everything it had accomplished. So America threw a party."

"The whole country threw a party?" Molly said. "Awesome! What kind of party? Where was it?"

"The party was called the Columbian Exposition," Veronica said. "In honor of Christopher Columbus. And as it happens it was held in Chicago. Chicago was one of America's great success stories at the time. The people of Chicago agreed to throw the party and they invited countries from all over the world to send them symbols of the world's achievements. Books, paintings, sculptures, machines – everyone wanted to send something to be on exhibit."

"And Lady Shelbourne sent the cups?"

"She did. She sent a whole exhibit on her father's railroads but first and foremost she sent the silver cups. She wanted to display something that would honor her father's hard work in the coal and railroad industries: silver Memorial Cups – the only anodized silver cups in the world. She couldn't tell people, of course, what the silver could be used for but she still wanted the world to see them. She made 14 cups, one for each of the seven seas and the seven continents, and she displayed them at the Columbian Exposition."

"Wow!" said Molly. Then she thought for a moment. "Wait a minute. 14 cups? But there were only 10 at Laurentide. Where are the others?"

"I have one," Veronica said. She reached into her courier bag and pulled out a memorial cup. Its silver gleamed in the light of the chandelier.

"Wow!" Molly marveled. "It's beautiful. But where are the others?"

"They're also safe," Veronica said, returning the cup to her bag.

"How do you know?"

"Because Mrs. Van Helsing has one and she has assured me it is safe. Another is at the Shelbourne estate in England and I am quite certain that one has not been touched. And the last, well, it is the safest of them all. It's at the White House."

"The White House?" Molly asked, shocked. "As in, *the* White House? Where the president lives?"

"Yes. When the Columbian Exposition ended in 1893 Lady Shelbourne gave one cup to President Grover Cleveland as a gift to the American people, to say thank you for the freedom America represents. It has been displayed in the White House ever since."

"No way," Molly said. "A silver cup is at the White House. A cup just like the ones at my school. Oh, my poor school..."

"That brings us back to our problem," Veronica continued. "Your school burned because of Ursula Bamcroft and her Pug-Nasties. But they don't belong in your time – how did they get there? They would have needed a train and they would have needed silver. A train they could steal, I suppose, but they must have found silver somewhere because there don't appear to be any missing cups."

"Are you sure?"

"We're as sure as we can be. I have mine, Isabelle has hers, and the Shelbourne estate would have let me know if theirs was missing. And of course the White House cup must be safe. It's not like you can just waltz into the White House whenever you want. I only saw it once but it was secure enough then."

"When was that?" Molly asked.

"In 1924," Veronica said.

Molly blinked. "In 1924?"

"Yes. It was at a party for President Calvin Coolidge's inauguration. Mr. Coolidge wasn't much of an entertainer and I was bored so I wandered into the other parlors. The cup was on display in the Green Room then."

Molly frowned. She was certain Veronica was pulling her leg.

"Whatever you say," she said. "But if a train needs silver in order to travel through time then either there is more silver somewhere or all the cups aren't safe. One of them must be missing."

Veronica nodded. "And if one is missing that means someone may be using it to create mischief. I am certain I know who that person is. But I don't know how to prove it or how to find her, so what we must do is return to the last place where all fourteen cups were together. That is especially important now that the ten Academy cups have been destroyed."

"But they haven't been," Molly said.

"I beg your pardon?"

"The cups weren't melted in the fire," Molly explained. "We saved them – but then the Pug-Nasties stole them from us." She told Veronica the whole story of her day, from the time she showed up at school until she arrived at the train station.

"Oh, dear," Veronica said when Molly finished. "That complicates things greatly. If the cups had been destroyed then at least they would be safe. But now they are in the very hands of the mischief-makers."

"I'm sorry. We tried to save them."

"Don't be sorry, Molly. You and your friends did a great deed."

Veronica thought some more. Finally, she announced: "I was wrong. Your information does not complicate things. In fact, this new development makes it more important than ever that we stick with my original plan. We must return to the last time the cups were together. That way we can collect them and keep them safe."

"And where was that?" Molly asked.

"Why, the Columbian Exposition of 1893, of course."

The door opened and Mr. Stewart returned.

"I have inspected every car and the *Jeremy Bentham* is in perfect order," he informed them. "Which is more than I can say for our voyage. Have you made a decision, Miss Veronica? Shall we cancel this journey now that it is out of our control?"

"Of course not, Mr. Stewart. We will continue."

"But it is an untimely journey! The Navigator has said we cannot control it."

"You said that *parts* of the journey are beyond our control," Veronica corrected the conductor. "That means we can control the rest. Control the things you can, I say, and deal with what you cannot. The first thing we can control is getting Molly cleaned up and out of that smoky school uniform. I will show you to your room, Molly, where there is a wash basin and bath. And there are clothes in the wardrobe that you can change into. Once you are presentable we will have a word with the Navigator. In the meantime, Mr. Stewart, please tell him to proceed as best he can."

Veronica led the way aft to the sleeping car. In it was a fancy bathroom with a copper tub, another chandelier, and pearl handles on the faucets. On the wash basin were exquisite packages of Larkin soaps. Next door were a dressing room and sleeping compartment.

"Bunk beds on a train! No way!" Molly cried. "Whoa! And look at these clothes..."

A wardrobe stretched across the compartment, filled with clothes of all colors and styles.

"Yes," said Veronica. "There are even more next door. It's quite a collection. For now may I recommend you wash up? I'll lay out something for you to wear tonight and tomorrow. I wasn't planning on 1952, exactly, but there should be something. If not, well...we'll improvise."

CHAPTER 11

—⁓—

Helpers

IMPROVISE, INDEED. WHEN Molly reappeared in the parlor car she wore a nightdress, slippers, and a flowery bathrobe that was three sizes too big.

"I look like a clown," she said. "Even my grandmother wouldn't wear this."

"Maybe your great-grandmother would," Veronica suggested. "I couldn't find any sleepwear from the 1950s but that robe was all the rage back in 1922. And anyway you can't wander the train in your nightgown. We must speak to the Navigator, so let's go."

The coach in front of the parlor car was divided into the kitchen galley and three offices. When Molly and Veronica entered it they stepped into the first office, a nearly empty room where a young man wearing suspenders sat at a table tapping away on a telegraph key. He leaped to his feet when they entered.

"Hello, Lewis," Veronica greeted him.

"Hello, Miss Veronica! Do you have a message for me to send?"

"No, not yet. Lewis, this is Molly. She'll accompany us on our journey."

"Hello, Molly. What a beautiful robe! Do you have a message for me to send?"

"What kind of message?" Molly asked.

"Any kind. I'm a certified telegrapher."

"A what?"

"A certified telegrapher. A Keyman 2nd Class. And I'm a member of the Order of Railroad Telegraphers," Lewis added proudly.

"What does that mean?"

"Lewis sends and collects messages," Veronica explained.

"Oh," Molly said. "Do you have a telephone?"

Lewis looked down his nose. "Of course not. Telephones are unreliable. We have a telegraph. It's as dependable as the first day it was used in 1844! Before the telegraph people had to use the Pony Express, where a message was passed from horse to horse. But then this little miracle changed everything."

He pointed to the telegraph key on the desk. It looked like a mousetrap with an arm on one side. When Molly pressed on the arm there was a satisfying *tap*.

"Everything on this train is old, isn't it?" she commented.

"But efficient," Lewis claimed. "Here, I'll show you."

He slid into his seat and tapped out a quick message in dots and dashes.

"There," he said happily. "I've sent a message to our dispatcher that you are on the train: *To Dispatch Office – stop – We confirm arrival at Laurentide – stop – Miss Molly safely on board – stop.*"

"Lewis, we don't have a dispatcher," Veronica reminded him gently.

Lewis' face fell. "But I can pretend," he insisted. "It gives me practice. And if you do have a message, Molly, I can send it wherever and whenever you would like."

"We'll think about that," Veronica promised. "Come along, Molly. Lewis, keep up the good work."

"Thank you, Miss Veronica. It's good to meet you, Molly. Remember, when you have a message, I'm your man!"

The girls moved on to the next office. In contrast to Lewis's orderly room, the Navigator's workplace was an explosion of paper. There were maps and diagrams everywhere: tacked to the walls, pinned to an easel, and even stuck to the ceiling. There were stacks of charts and schedules and on a desk a great mound of paper was in the process of sliding off onto the floor. A speaking tube ran along the wall above a scratch pad where one handwritten note after another was crossed off. In the middle of it all was a portly man with curly hair and eyeglasses perched on his nose. He rushed from one map to another muttering to himself.

"...the most ridiculous thing I've ever heard...The Cedar Rapids line is always open this time of year...late snowfall my big toe... Rock Island to Memphis to St. Louis...no, that won't work...Track 47B is under construction and the siding is closed...But wait, the Cuyahoga bridge!" He ran to a timetable. "Oh, no. That won't work either...."

"Good evening, Mr. Magellan," Veronica greeted the man.

"Oh, hello, Miss Veronica. Forgive the mess...very busy here, very busy. Lots of changes, lots to do. This untimely business has thrown a fly into the ointment, if you know what I mean. Quite a number of flies, actually, ha-ha! A wrench in the works, a spanner in the spokes, that sort of thing." Mr. Magellan sorted through the catalogues on his desk. "Trains run on schedule, you know, and we are not on schedule. Very inconvenient, this."

"Yes, Mr. Magellan. I understand we are a minute early but surely you'll be able to make up the time somewhere..."

"Make up the time?" Mr. Magellan came around the desk and looked Molly in the face. "Did you hear what she said? Ha! One does not simply 'make up time' like it's a hasty pudding one throws together for tea! Time is not created whenever one needs it and then tossed away when you're done. Time *is*, my dear. It is what it is and it is what you do with it. Well, what we've done with it is we've messed with it, I'll tell you what. We've departed a minute early – now we're traveling through history out of step with everyone else. Do you dance, young lady?"

"Huh?" said Molly.

"Do you dance? You know, trip the light fantastic, beat the boards, caper across the stage, that sort of thing? The foxtrot, the waltz, the Peabody perhaps?" Mr. Magellan leaped around the room like a teddy bear doing ballet.

"Sometimes my girlfriends and I dance at school," Molly admitted.

"That's perfect then! So you'll understand. We left the station a minute early and are now trying to travel on railroads out of step with every other train. We're like a dancer crossing the floor three beats off from everyone else. Do you know what happens when you do that? *Kaplooey!*" he cried, smacking his hands together. "Collisions, crashes, mayhem, disaster! We can't have that, can we?"

"Oh, no!"

"No, indeed. We would cause untold damage through the last two centuries. Mayhem is not permitted. Not while I am the Navigator."

"But Mr. Magellan," Veronica interrupted. "I had planned for this to be a simple journey back to the Exposition."

"A simple journey? Miss Veronica, don't make a stuffed bird laugh! There is no way this will be a simple journey."

"And why not?"

"Why not? Are you daft?" The Navigator jumped onto a chair and waved his arms. "Because of what I just said! To travel anywhere we must travel on existing rail lines. Rail lines that existed in every year through which we are traveling. But we're no longer a scheduled train! So to travel anywhere we must find the railroads that *are* available at any given moment in history and use those, then look for others to connect to. Look about you! Do you think I always decorate my office this way?"

Molly stepped to the easel and studied the papers there. "Is this a map?" she asked.

Mr. Magellan rushed over. He ran his hands across the paper as though it were a work of art.

"Not at all. What you are looking at is a timetable for the Chesapeake and Ohio Railway. A horse blanket, it's called, because of the gorgeous colors. Look at these lines! Only given to railroad employees, it was. It shows every train scheduled to run each year, what track it will run on, and at what time. Such organization, such planning...it's *beautiful*, really orderly. I was using it to get us through the 1970s and 1960s. But here, see these rails and these stations? Starting in the 1950s everything is booked solid. Trains were popular then, you know, and finding open lines is much more difficult before 1962. It's like trying to slip into traffic during rush hour."

"But that is unacceptable, Mr. Magellan," Veronica stated. "We must get to the Exposition."

"Unacceptable?" Mr. Magellan exclaimed. "Of course, it's unacceptable! But it's not like walking across the street, you know. When you cross the street you travel in a straight line and that's what we do, too, on a normal journey of the *Jeremy Bentham*. We travel through history in a straight line. But now a straight line is the last thing we can do. We would crash into trains left and right and cause unimaginable horrible things. It's right out. Not an option. Can't do it. Forget about it. There is no way to get to the Exposition. No way. Houdini himself could not find us a way. It's *impossible*."

"Impossible, Mr. Magellan?" Veronica repeated.

"Impossible!"

Veronica T. Boone raised an eyebrow and crossed her arms.

Mr. Magellan took a breath. He wiped his forehead and looked around the room in despair. "Well, look," he sighed. "A *straight* line is in fact impossible. I've been trying to find one to the 19th century and it doesn't exist. But maybe there is another way. We could take detours."

"Detours?" Veronica asked.

"Yes. We could re-route from one track to another. For example, instead of going right to the Exposition in 1893, we go first to Chicago in 1952. That I can do – I've already found us an open line on the old Indiana Eastern Railway. It wasn't hard: the tracks between now and then are fairly clear since folks pretty much stopped riding trains after the 1960s."

"But what will we do in 1952?" Veronica asked in amazement.

"I don't know," the Navigator squealed. "I can't tell you how to use your time. I can only get you there and give you the opportunity to do something productive while I find us another track to ride on."

"Another track to where?"

"Who knows? Maybe to Rochester or Dubuque or even Timbuktu! We'll have to accept whatever track is open."

"But I haven't planned on all those stops," Veronica pointed out.

"Neither have I, Miss Veronica. But we have no choice. Now, it will take me some time to go through all this mess and find a route to the Exposition. You'll simply have to adjust."

Veronica T. Boone thought about that. She looked at the maps as though one of them would leap up and offer her a solution. None of them did.

"Very well, Mr. Magellan," she said finally. "You are the Navigator. We will trust you to find us a way."

"Of course, Miss Veronica. I have never failed you, have I?"

"No, Mr. Magellan, you have not. Lord Shelbourne chose you above all others to navigate the *Jeremy Bentham* on its journeys. He said if there was anyone who could chart a path in difficult times, it was you. Since Lord Shelbourne trusted you, I will, too."

Mr. Magellan swelled with pride. "I will not disappoint you, miss. But..." he looked around the mess in his office, "it will take time."

Veronica stepped over a stack of train schedules to reach the door. "Mr. Magellan," she said. "Time is one thing we have. And to ensure we use it wisely we will speak to your neighbor. Come along, Molly."

The last room in the coach was not as spare as Lewis' office nor was it chaotic like the Navigator's room. It was a library.

There were bookcases from floor to ceiling on every wall. In fact, the door that Veronica and Molly entered through was a bookcase itself: when they closed it behind them they could no longer see where they had entered. The books on the shelves were large with firm covers.

A distinguished gentleman sat reading in a comfy chair. He wore a velvet jacket, an Oxford shirt, a silk kerchief, dress trousers, and lambskin slippers over argyle socks. He smoked a pipe and next to him on a table were a cup of tea and a dish of crackers.

"Ah, good evening, Veronica," the gentleman greeted them. "Do forgive us for not standing. These books are so heavy... Care for a crisp?" He held out a cracker.

"Oh, no, Professor, thank you. And please don't get up," Veronica replied. To Molly she whispered, "I've never seen him get out of that chair. And he always refers to himself as *we*."

"And who is this with you?"

"Professor Cooke, this is Molly. She is a student at Laurentide Academy and has agreed to travel with us a while. There is trouble brewing."

"Oh, dear," said Professor Cooke. "Not Ursula Bamcroft again."

"I'm afraid so."

"Oh, what a pain that woman is. A thoroughly duplicitous person, always frowning and talking about fairness but behind it all just wanting to take from people what is rightfully theirs. They never learn, these people. Always angry. Always bitter. But how can we help, my dear?"

"Well, Professor. My plan had been to return to the Exposition and recover the silver. Without the silver Ursula cannot travel, and if she cannot travel she cannot cause the problems she has, such as burning down Molly's town."

"Burning down your town?" the professor exclaimed. "How barbaric. How very socialist. That sounds like something the Wobblies would do."

"What are Wobblies?" Molly asked.

"Thugs," the professor replied. "Wobblies are thugs. Barbarians who destroy factories and stores and houses if they don't get what they want. We have their whole history right here," he pointed to a bookshelf near his chair. "We know who they are and where they went and where they lived and when."

"Wow," said Molly. "You must read a lot."

"Why, yes! That is what we do," the professor smiled.

"The professor reads everything," Veronica said with pride. "No one knows more history than he does. He is a wonderful source of information which is why he is on the *Jeremy Bentham*."

"And how may we be of service today, Veronica?" Professor Cooke asked. "There must be something afoot."

"Quite so," Veronica agreed. "We are on an untimely journey, Professor, and it is very likely we will need your advice."

"An untimely journey, you say?" The professor closed his book and crossed his legs. "Well, that is unusual. We've not been on one of those. We daresay we have not even heard of one of those..." He scanned his bookshelves as though they had let him down.

"None of us have," Veronica told him. "It was my intention to return directly to the Columbian Exposition of 1893 and deal with Ursula Bamcroft there. However, the Navigator informs us that is out of the question due to our early departure from Laurentide. It appears we must now reach the Exposition in a haphazard fashion, by leaping from one rail line to the next, one year to the next."

"The Navigator," Professor Cooke scoffed. "That near-sighted potato sack of poppycock. He wouldn't know how to read a railroad schedule if it bit him on the nose."

A panel on the wall slid open and Mr. Magellan's face filled the opening.

"I heard that!" he snapped. "You lazy old coot. I know every railroad from Sheffield to San Francisco, from Dover to Detroit. If you would ever get your bottom out of that chair and your nose out of those books, you would see how a real researcher works!"

"Real researcher, indeed. You're not worthy of the name, you backwater blockhead!" Professor Cooke threw a cracker at the wall panel but the Navigator slid it shut just in time.

"They're really good friends," Veronica whispered to Molly. "They just like to argue."

"Ahem," Professor Cooke said, recovering his composure. "If we will be stopping on our way to 1893, we imagine you will want some advice."

"That is correct, Professor. We'll have time on each detour – maybe a little, maybe more. As you know we should never waste time, so I was wondering if you would do some research before each of our stops. Then perhaps you could help us make things right."

Professor Cooke puffed happily on his pipe. "Of course, we will help," he cried. "We *love* doing research. We *love* learning. We will scan the entire library twice over if necessary to help you." He tapped his nose and pointed at Molly. "The whole world is contained in books, my dear child. Remember that. The best friend you will ever have is a book, and the next best friend will also be a book." He settled deep into his chair and looked about the room like a child on Christmas, wondering which volume to pull from the shelves first.

"Thank you, Professor," Veronica said, swinging open the hidden door. "I knew that, as always, you would be indispensable in our time of need."

"It is our pleasure, dear girl," the professor trilled, blowing rings of smoke. "Just tell that nincompoop Navigator to keep us informed and we will in turn ensure you know all you need."

"I heard that!" the Navigator yelled from next door, just before Veronica swung the door shut.

On the way back to their bunks the girls passed through the parlor car where Molly looked around and scratched her head.

"Is anything wrong?" Veronica asked.

"Oh, my brain is as tired as the rest of me," Molly sighed, picking up Peter's backpack and looking underneath it, then searching around the dining table. "I thought I put one of the cucumber sandwiches aside for a late-night snack but it's not here now."

"Are you still hungry?" Veronica asked. "Do you want to call Higgins?"

"Oh, no. I don't want to bother him. Right now I just want to go to bed. It's been the longest day of my life and I'm exhausted."

"That is a good idea," Veronica agreed. "I don't know how long we'll be in Chicago tomorrow but it's a big city. We will need our energy."

Molly did need to rest. She crawled into her bunk bed and dozed immediately, lulled by the gentle *clackety-clack* of the wheels below as the *Jeremy Bentham* raced over the steel rails. But just as she was about to drift off to sleep, she sat up.

"A message!" she exclaimed. "Of course I need to send a message!"

She jumped from her bunk and raced out the door, wrapping the robe around her. Through the parlor car she hurried, straight into Lewis' office.

"Lewis, I do need you to send a message," she announced.

Lewis was so happy he looked ready to burst. "At your service!" he cried. "To whom, to where, and to when?"

"To my Aunt Marcy," Molly explained. "In Laurentide. Or maybe in Wavering – I don't know. She and my brother Michael escaped the fire on the ferry. I was supposed to go with her and she's probably worried sick now because I didn't get there. Right away, please. Tell her I'm okay and...well, I don't know when I'll be back, but I'll be back as soon as I can."

"Of course you will," Lewis assured her. "Miss Veronica is always very good about that. If I know her, she'll return you as soon as you left. And don't worry about your message. I'll send it by telegram tomorrow as soon as we arrive in Chicago. And I'll expedite it at no extra charge – we'll make it a *FLASH PARTICULAR* so it gets priority." Lewis rubbed his hands in excitement. "I've never sent a *FLASH PARTICULAR* before. But that way your Aunt Marcy will receive your message yesterday and she'll have nothing to worry about when she gets on the boat today."

Molly scratched her head. "I don't understand. You're going to send a message tomorrow that my Aunt Marcy will get yesterday?"

"Why yes. It costs more but most people find it's worth the money."

"Well, whatever you say. You're the professional. Me, I'm going to bed. So much of this day has made no sense to me at all. Maybe tomorrow will be better."

Lewis laughed. "Don't count on that. But get a good night's sleep, Miss Molly. We'll see you tomorrow. And don't worry about your message. You can trust a Keyman 2nd Class to see it through."

"Thank you, Lewis. Good night."

Molly returned to her compartment and climbed into her bunk. Veronica was already asleep. It was only a moment before Molly was dozing again, too. She was so tired that even in her dreams she was sleeping, rocking back and forth and listening to a distant train whistle wail in the night. Clouds formed and fog rose about the train. Somewhere down the tracks was Chicago though they couldn't see it yet. Molly slept and slept as the *Jeremy Bentham* rolled through the night.

~

Never fear!
The Untimely Journey of Veronica T. Boone
continues in
Part 2: The Jeremy Bentham
- available now!

About the Author

D. M. Sears lives and writes in Virginia. He is a pilot who has traveled the world, flown on six continents, and written several books about airplanes under the name Michael Bleriot. *The Untimely Journey of Veronica T. Boone* was born when his niece requested an adventure story for a 12-year-old girl, one that included trains, horses, and Chicago's Museum of Science and Industry. She said it should also include the history of America, "but only the interesting parts."

CPSIA information can be obtained
at www.ICGtesting.com
Printed in the USA
LVHW081450110821
695075LV00019B/310

9 780996 231510